THIS NIGHT WOUNDS TIME

The Mysterious Disappearances of Stacie Madison and Susan Smalley

D1706613

Shawn Sutherland

Selected photographs by Laura Marie Jimenez

For Stacie and Susan

This Night Wounds Time
© 2009 by Shawn Sutherland

Cover design by Al Ridenour

Selected photographs by Laura Marie Jimenez

ISBN 978-0-557-20045-0

Printed in the United States of America

A NOTE ABOUT THE TITLE OF THIS BOOK

In 1974, the British rock band King Crimson released its classic album *Starless and Bible Black*. (The album's title is a reference to Dylan Thomas' play *Under Milkwood*.) Featuring not only a stellar performance by John Wetton – the future bassist and vocalist for 1980s super group Asia – the album's back cover includes a close-up of a section of painter Tom Phillips' 1970 masterpiece *A Humument*.

The album's graphic is an explosive swirl of black, red, white and pale blue surrounding four ominous words - "this night wounds time."

Although once ignorant to the meaning of this cryptic phrase, in researching and drafting this book, I have come to understand all too well its import and impact.

Time is ultimately that place within the human psyche where hopes regarding the future, concerns for the present, and memories of things past reside in tandem. If ever there was a night in which time was forever wounded, it was the night on which Stacie Madison and Susan Smalley disappeared.

The girls' community has never been the same and, in the 21 years that have elapsed since March 20, 1988, Stacie's and Susan's families have existed in the inescapable shadow of a mystery that remains unsolved. Their lives are unjustly and irrevocably altered by the unexplained events of that night.

Carolyn, Ida, John Richard, Rich, Sara and Stefanie: may "the Lord turn his face toward you and give you peace."[1]

Shawn Sutherland
Richardson, Texas

---

1 Numbers 6:26 (New International Version).

ACKNOWLEDGEMENTS

This book would not have been possible had it not been for the kind indulgences of following individuals and entities:

Marilyn Hutchison
Ida Madison
Stefanie Madison
Carolyn Smalley
John Richard Smalley
Rich Smalley

David W. Bock
Sergeant John W. Crawford (Carrollton Police Department)
Sergeant Joel F. Payne (Carrollton Police Department)
Ohlen L. Sapp
Woody Specht (Carrollton Police Department)
Assistant Chief Monty Stanley (Carrollton Police Department)
Captain Greg Ward (Frisco Police Department)

David Abbey
Michael Alexander
Paula Thomas Allen
Lori Pepsis Baker
Marisa Barrier
Greg Batchelor
Kelli Hargrove Barton
Mark Blythe
Carol Lynn Cowan Bockes
Jon Bohls
Bobby Brannon
Stefanie Brown
David Culp
Robin Hohner Devenish
C. Kenneth Dockray
Jill J. Farrer
Lisa Allen Foley
Meredith Foster
Laurie Lillback Gage
Sheryl Rummans Giles
Laura Glaser
Rich Guerra
Robert Hembree
Roger & Abby Holmes (North Dallas Antique Mall)
Michelle Bolig Huber
Andrew Jayroe

Samantha Judge
Shana Hearon Ladd
Kitty LaDouce
Michael W. Leach
Helga Dannheim Lewenberg
Litigation Solution, Inc.
Lonnie Lutz
Tom Mackey
Steve Manderfeld
John McCaa
Jennifer DeVoe McCord
Laura Miller
Shannon Moller
Cathy Carrell Parker
Joe Pouncy
Bryan Pruner
Philip Dean Ringley, Jr.
Crystal Rainwater-Roberson
Stacy Robinson
Michelle Rhone
Amy Cloninger Schomerus
Stacey Allmon Simpson
Deanna Bowman Sinclair
Paul Joseph Smith
Sheryl Maguire Steger
Angie Kaneshiro Stevens
Patty Stevens
Paul V. Storm
Storm LLP
Sarah Stutsman
Surrey Cafe
Judy Steger Sutherland
Shanan Tepecik
Michael VanVickle
Georgeanne Elder Villard
Karen Volchok
Kelly Driskell Wells
Susan Lott Wheeler
Melody Sutton Whipple
Julee White (Brinker International)
Heidi Monk Wilhelm
Edward L. Williams
Karen Wisdom
Toni McNamara Wylie

Special thanks to: Laura Marie Jimenez for providing many of this book's photographs, including several images of the various restaurants on Forest Lane which could not be included herein owing to copyright obstacles; Al Ridenour for designing the cover art; and Ida Madison, Anthony P. Miller, Mark D. Perdue, Karen Roper, Curt Rowlett, Rich Smalley and Pat Wallis for proofing, editing and otherwise critiquing the pages of this manuscript.

I am grateful to Arby's Restaurant Group, Inc. for graciously granting me permission to include images of their establishment in this book when several other corporations with restaurants on Forest Lane would not.

Special thanks must be extended to the Carrollton Police Department as a whole. In this regard, I must emphasize that, unlike the caricatures one sees in movies of obstructionist police officers intent on thwarting a writer's access to information, inasmuch as its internal regulations allowed, the Carrollton Police Department could not have been more accommodating to my requests for information and insights, and they seemingly went out of their way to assist me in my endeavors. For this, I am eternally grateful.

Finally, I am grateful to my wife, Judy, for tolerating my near eight month total immersion in this story and for abiding the fact that, for much of 2009, my thoughts were all too often lost somewhere on the winds of 1988.

Shawn Sutherland
Richardson, Texas

CHAPTER INDEX

	Preface	i
1	Who Am I to Tell This Story?	1
2	Sunday, March 20, 1988	8
3	Monday, March 21, 1988	12
4	Stacie	14
5	Sapp and Bock	32
6	Everybody Turns Out Fine	34
7	The Ford Mustang	39
8	Susan	46
9	No Blame on the Carrollton Police Department	59
10	Carrollton Police Ask For Help	66
11	The City of Carrollton	68
12	I Really Miss That	77
13	Once Upon a Time on Forest Lane	85
14	Bad Dreams	99
15	Reconstructing the Night	101
16	Speculation and Theories	117
17	Jason Lawton, Suspect	121
18	Aftershocks	133
19	The Time Is Now	143
20	Alternate Realities	149
21	Since I Last Kissed You Goodbye	153
	Bibliography	155
	About the Author	158

PREFACE

In the earliest days of this endeavor, I informed a literary agent with whom I have been working on another project that my plan was to spend the summer of 2009 creating the book you now hold in your hands.

My vision was, I said, to tell the story of the as yet unsolved mysterious disappearances of Stacie Madison and Susan Smalley, two seniors at Newman Smith High School in Carrollton, Texas, who vanished on March 20, 1988.

I stated that my hope was – by weaving a story that examined the known facts of the case and the impact it continues to have on the Carrollton/Farmers Branch community – the book might move the individuals who know the truth about the girls' fates to finally break their silence.

I was quickly informed that what I envisioned would be nearly impossible to sell to a mainstream publisher for a number of reasons.

For one thing, the girls were never national news or household names.

A bigger obstacle, though, was that, since it is the story of a cold case, the book would be minus an ending. And the public, or so I am told, is prone to avoid reading about unsolved mysteries unless they are of the most garish sort, such as the Black Dahlia, Jack the Ripper or the Zodiac. I would later learn that the higher profile television programs devoted to capturing criminals had also declined for years to broadcast the details of the Madison/Smalley case because police lack a suspect whose photograph they can publicize.

The equation is a simple one: solved mysteries are revisited by the media *ad nauseam* while cold cases – the ones truly needing exposure – languish. This was the epitome of irony, only it was not the least bit funny.

With this project shot down in flames by a representative of the publishing world, I found myself more determined than ever to get the story of Stacie Madison and Susan Smalley before the public. I determined that if self-publishing was my only option until a mainstream publisher decided to option the book, so be it. And if the book went unnoticed by other presses, I could live with that too. In the interim, I would use the vanity presses to my advantage and offer the book at the lowest price imaginable in order to ensure that the story reached the largest audience possible.

This book, then, is the result of my resolve.

1

WHO AM I TO TELL THIS STORY?

I did not even have to wonder whose story I was supposed to tell.

On a frigid night in the early months of 1988, my girlfriend and I, along with my mother, braved the cold to travel to a steakhouse in Carrollton, Texas.

At that time, I was 24 years old and bore – or so I had convinced myself – the weight of the world on my shoulders.

I was 15 months sober but barely understood that there was so much more to this term than simply not drinking. A lifetime before, in October 1986, the Christian college in which I was enrolled had decided it could continue just fine without me and my alcohol-related infractions and had sent me packing.

Re-enrolled in that same college, I was now working hard to right my life that had once been in a tailspin, and getting ready to complete my final semester.

A sunny future, however, was not necessarily in the forecast. Instead, a funk had descended upon me weeks earlier as I became evermore (erroneously) convinced that the liberal arts degree which would soon be mine was going to equip me to do little more than become a shoe salesman.

This dread was ever present, ever unwelcome.

That was where my mind was.

A CONTAGIOUS SMILE

Once at the restaurant, my mood was shattered as if by magic.

There I encountered a presence which made me forget about the dreaded future. It was a familiar face asking me how many people there were in our dinner party. It was a face that I recognized as the adult incarnation of one I had known years before – one belonging to a child who had shopped at the K-Mart where I had once worked. Yet here she was now – a woman in her own right. Oddly, realizing that this child had grown into an adult filled me with an odd sense of joy. It affirmed that, no matter how preoccupied we might become with its details, the cycle of life is unstoppable.

THIS NIGHT WOUNDS TIME

To this day, I cannot recall the Carrollton-related small talk this young woman and I exchanged while I waited to be seated for dinner. Regardless, recognizing her face and spending a few moments talking with her had lifted me out of the melancholy in which I had found myself for weeks and served to remind me that there was more to life, and more to me, than professors, grades, tests, graduation, and the hope of finding a job. It was just one of those simple moments in life when another person's smile and mood was contagious.

SPRING BREAK 1988

Weeks later, during Spring Break 1988, I distracted myself with sleeping late, writing letters to family and friends, reading forgettable books, soaking up as much sunshine as possible and watching reruns of television programs I had already seen countless times too many.

I remember absolutely nothing specific about Spring Break that year except for a story that ran on the local evening news in the middle of the week announcing that local police were reaching out to viewers for assistance in determining what had become of two seniors at Carrollton's Newman Smith High School who had disappeared days before.

At the mention of the words "Newman Smith," my ears had perked up. Beginning in the 8th Grade, I had spent 1977 through 1982, five years of my life, walking the halls of that campus.

The two girls, the story reported, were last seen sometime between 12:45 a.m. and 1:30 a.m. on Sunday, March 20, when one of them stopped in to visit a co-worker at the steakhouse in Addison where she worked as a hostess.

Beyond the Newman Smith connection, the story meant little to me.

CYNICISM

Somehow I never caught sight of the girls' photographs on television or in the newspapers that week. As well, as did many, I presumed the pair had probably disappeared by choice in order to partake of the ongoing partying at South Padre Island, which was the rage at the time.

Ever cynical at that point in my life, I predicted to friends that the two girls would probably show up on the news again in a day or two – bearing marks on their backsides administered by their parents who had paddled them for running off and putting everyone through torment.

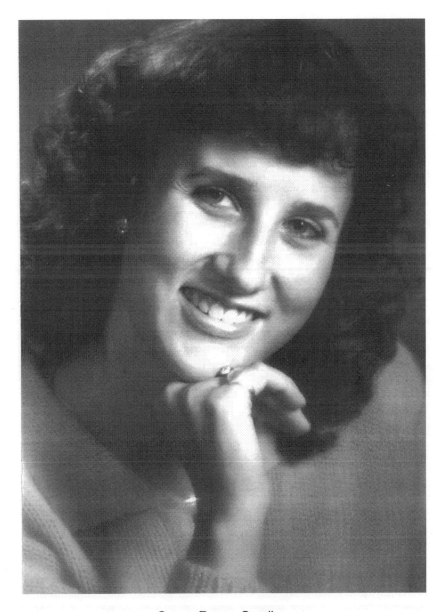

Susan Renee Smalley
(Photo courtesy of Rich Smalley)

THIS NIGHT WOUNDS TIME

CERTAIN OF THEIR RETURN

Spring Break came to a close on Sunday and, as I began packing for my drive back to school, I thought of the girls. Surely they would return to their families later that day with sheepish looks on their faces. That did not happen. I returned to college, graduated a few weeks later, moved to Houston and largely forgot about the two girls.

Then I saw the missing poster.

THE MISSING POSTER

It was in the parking lot of a Dallas shopping center.
Night had fallen.
It was the fall of the year and there was a chill in the air.
The rain was falling hard.
I was in Dallas from Houston visiting family and friends, and we had gone to eat in a restaurant.

As we pulled into the restaurant's parking lot, someone in the car I was driving mentioned that one of the posters regarding the two missing girls, which had been distributed by the hundreds, was tacked to a nearby telephone pole. A reward for information leading to the recovery of the two girls was being offered. Merchants gladly posted the missing posters in their shop windows, and the girls were still periodically mentioned in Dallas area newspapers.

My curiosity took hold of me.

Wanting to see just who these two individuals were that had created such widespread emotions, I edged my car closer to the telephone pole and rolled down my car's window in order to get a closer look at the fading poster.

THAT SAME CONTAGIOUS SMILE

What I saw made my heart stop. Staring back at me from that piece of paper was a blonde I did not recognize. The other face, though, I knew instantly. The smile was unmistakable. It was the same one that had lifted my spirits that freezing cold night earlier in the year.

A girl from Carrollton, Texas...a hostess at a local steakhouse...a student at Newman Smith High School...how had I failed to connect the dots? With rain beating me in the face, I sat in stunned silence. A hypothetical story, from which I was a million miles detached, about two girls from Carrollton disappearing had impacted me little. But a single piece of paper changed everything. I had spoken to this girl at whose image I was now staring. It was like a ton of bricks had crushed me. I was speechless. It was as if something had been

4

stolen from me.

FAST FORWARD

In the years that followed, I eventually returned to Dallas and found a good career.

Every so often my mind found its way back to the story of "those two girls," as they eventually came to be known in Carrollton mythology. In those moments, I thought of their families – whom I did not know – and wondered how they were coping.

In one such moment, via an old newspaper, I learned the girls' names: the blonde was Stacie Elisabeth Madison and the brunette to whom I had spoken years before was Susan Renee Smalley.

Affixing names to their faces seemed only to intensify the extent to which the story of their unsolved disappearances disturbed me. Quite simply, I could not comprehend the truth that two people from my hometown had vanished as if they had never existed.

Quite often, thoughts of the girls would come to me in the deep, dark hours of the night.

Most often, "They're still missing" would be my thoughts on the girls, and of their unrepentant and unpunished abductors I would think, "They're still out there."

I would ponder what it would take for police to crack the case, namely a confession, and grow frustrated.

Eventually, this anger would evaporate until it found its way to me again. Then it began.

TELL THEIR STORY

"Tell their story." It was 2008, and I awoke in the middle of the night with those three words pounding in my head. "Tell their story." It was as if, while I slept, that admonition had been stenciled on my brain. "Tell their story." Definitions of the New Testament term "Holy Spirit" vary. In my life, it is the empowering hand of God that guides my life and oftentimes directs me down pathways I could never imagine. This time it had found a function for my fury and was whispering its instructions to me. "Tell their story." I did not even have to wonder whose story I was supposed to tell. I knew.

WHERE TO BEGIN?

Oddly, I was not afraid.

I knew this was a story I could tell, but doing so properly would require cooperation from the Madisons and Smalleys. And just how in the world would I go about gaining that?

5

I was not fearful of contacting the girls' families. While collecting material for my book on California cult leader Krishna Venta (born Francis Pencovic) I had overcome any trepidation I ever had about making contact with people out of the clear blue. In actuality, while researching that book, I had even become friends with a number of those closest to the man. But this situation was something entirely different.

The Madison and Smalley families probably had as many questions as I did about the girls' disappearances, and chances were they were not going to appreciate some stranger requesting permission to poke around into their private lives.

"Tell their story."

Those three words would not allow me to let go of the quest.

The only thing I could think to do was to try and contact the families, be as honest with them as I could, try to convey to them my passion for Stacie's and Susan's stories, explain my ideas regarding what I envisioned and attempt to explain my inspiration for writing this story without sounding like a madman.

CONTACT MADE

With the help of an internet community touted as a "social utility that connects people," I eventually got word to the girls' families in the spring of 2009.

In my missive I told them everything, including that night at the restaurant 21 years earlier when Susan had seated us, my remembrances of Spring Break 1988, my reaction to the missing poster and my conviction that I was being called to write this book.

Fearing more than ever that I might be perceived as a ghoul by the families, I closed my letter with the promise that I would do nothing until I heard from them and that I would abandon the project immediately if they even remotely viewed it as an exercise in bad taste.

PERMISSION GRANTED

I did not have to wait long for my answers.

Within days of sending my communiqué, I received a response from Ida Madison, Stacie's mother, saying, "Based on the information in your letter…I can only give you my approval for such a project."[1]

A few days later, Rich Smalley, Susan's brother, wrote to me also to say, "We think the book will be good as long as it is done with

---

1 Ida Madison, May 3, 2009.

respect and dignity towards the girls."[2]

A DAUNTING TASK

There it was. My requests for the families' respective trusts had been granted and I was determined not to misuse it. For days, I had braced myself for the likelihood that Stacie's and Susan's families would simply be too press shy after so many years and tell me "Thanks, but no thanks." They did not know me at all. But here I was, entrusted by two families, both hurt by time in ways I could not even imagine, with telling the stories of their lost loved ones.

For the first time, I was afraid. Who was I to tell this story?

---

2 Rich Smalley, May 12, 2009.

2

SUNDAY, MARCH 20, 1988

"How will you know if we're there?"

When the clock on her kitchen wall began inching towards 3:00 p.m., Ida Madison knew in her heart that something was dreadfully wrong. It was a sensation only a mother could experience or understand.

Ida's 17 year old daughter Stacie was now nearly an hour late in arriving home, and it was simply not like her to be late, even by an hour, without calling to offer some explanation. This was particularly true since today, March 20, 1988, was the last day of Spring Break, and Stacie had things she had to do before school resumed the next day.

RECALLING THE EVENTS OF SATURDAY

When she left the previous afternoon to go spend the night with a friend, a girl named Susan Smalley, Stacie had indicated she would be home on Sunday afternoon by 2:00 p.m. at the latest. Granted, she was now late by only one hour, but something about the day just did not feel right to Ida.

A woman meticulous enough to pursue in-depth genealogical research in libraries long before the advent of the internet, 43 year old Ida began replaying in her head the details of the previous day.

THE MORNING

Stacie had gotten up early, very early, on Saturday morning, March 19, 1988 in order to take the Standard Aptitude Test (SAT). A senior at Newman Smith High School in Carrollton, Texas, Stacie was an honor roll student and excited about taking business classes in the fall at what was then North Texas State University.

After the test, Ida had given Stacie a home perm.

SUSAN

As Stacie waited to rinse the perm solution from her hair, the phone rang. On the other end of the line was Stacie's friend, Susan, calling to see if Stacie wanted to spend the night at her house.

Susan and Stacie had met one another the previous semester when the two had shared a vocational education class. Since that time, the two had become close friends and were often together.

So, just where could they be now?

BECAUSE YOU NEVER KNOW WHEN I'LL CALL

Ida, a substitute school teacher, continued with her mental play by play of the previous day, resuming from the point at which Stacie washed the perm solution from her hair. She had then dressed in a white sweatshirt (with "American Business Women's Competition" emblazoned across its front), white pants and white sneakers. Then Susan arrived. That was shortly after 5:00 p.m.

In the final days of this book project, I discovered a previously unknown detail concerning March 19, 1988. A third girl, a friend of Susan's named Deanna Bowman, says she had intended to "hang out" with Stacie and Susan that evening, but a family birthday had thrown a wrench into her plans.[1] Stacie and Susan would be a twosome that Saturday night.

The two girls were apparently ready for the evening to begin and wasted little time with small talk before heading toward the Madison's front door.

On their way out, Ida called to Stacie and told her that, even though she was spending the night away from home, her midnight curfew still applied. "How will you know if we're there?" one of the girls jokingly asked. The question, although offered in jest, was met by a serious retort from Ida: "Because you never know when I'll call."[2]

The girls then loaded Stacie's overnight bag and hot rollers into the backseat of her Mustang and headed out for the evening. Susan was driving her mother's car, and Stacie followed in her car as the two headed toward the Smalley's condominium.

When the girls pulled away, Frank Madison, a cable repairman for Southwestern Bell Telephone Co., to whom Ida had been married for 20 years, was tinkering on one of the family cars. In so doing, he had missed the opportunity to tell his daughter goodbye when she left.

That was now nearly 24 hours ago, and Ida just could not get beyond the unsettling feeling that something bad had happened to the girls.

---

1 Deanna Bowman Sinclair, September 28, 2009.
2 "Little revealed in decade since 2 teens vanished," *The Fort Worth Star-Telegram*, March 18, 1998.

PRETTY RESPONSIBLE AND INDEPENDENT

Reaching for the telephone, Ida dialed Susan's telephone number. Susan's mother, Carolyn, answered the phone.

No, the girls were not there, Carolyn told Ida.

Her presumption was that, since it was such a pretty day, the girls were probably just out, enjoying the afternoon.[3]

At that point in time, Carolyn, a single mom who worked both a full-time job with an insurance company and part-time in a retail department store, was not worried – yet.

"She was concerned, but she knew that Susan was responsible. She was 18. She was an adult," observed Susan's brother, Rich Smalley, as he recalled his mother's somewhat calm demeanor on Sunday, March 20, 1988.

Earlier that afternoon, Carolyn had called Rich to express her mounting concerns about having not heard from Susan since the previous evening. Still, she did not yet fear the worst.

"We [Susan and Rich] were both pretty responsible and independent people...my mother just knew Susan's character and what she'd done in the past...she'd always been responsible...my Mom had confidence in Susan, and her mannerisms, and her sense of responsibility."[4]

This observation mirrors Carolyn's own words from 2001, when she told a reporter from the *The Dallas Morning News*, "Susan was 18 then, and she had always been a good kid. So I'd never given her a real strict curfew.[5] Stacie's curfew, though, had always been extremely regimented. And according to its standards, she was now very late.

TRYING NOT TO PACE

Ida tried not to pace, but she kept finding herself returning to the front window and watching for Stacie's car. A temporary reprieve from Ida's fears came around 6:00 p.m., when her mother called suggesting that she, Ida, Frank and their other two daughters, 14 year old Sara and six year old Stefanie, go to dinner at a nearby restaurant.

Hoping Stacie might be home when the family returned from dinner, Ida left her a note saying where they had gone and when they expected to be back. When the family arrived home a couple of hours later, they discovered the note in the same place where Ida had

---

3 Carolyn Smalley, July 14, 2009.
4 Rich Smalley, June 27, 2009.
5 Michael Granberry, "Vanished without a trace – 13 years after teens disappeared, families still wait, wonder," *The Dallas Morning News*, August 19, 2001.

placed it. Stacie was still not home, and night was falling. That was when the panic began. Ida returned to replaying the events of Saturday in her head.

Was there anything she had forgotten that might explain where Stacie was? Literally unable to sit still, Ida began telephoning everyone she knew in the hopes that someone had perhaps seen Stacie or knew where she might be. No one had any answers, not even Stacie's best friends or the boy she had been dating.

STACIE'S BOYFRIEND – JASON LAWTON

Until that moment, Ida had forgotten that Stacie's boyfriend, "Jason Lawton,"[6] had called the previous evening around 11:00 p.m. and asked to speak with Stacie. On her way out the door the previous day, Stacie had instructed her mother to tell Jason, should he call, that she was spending the night with Susan. So, when he telephoned, says Ida, "I told him she was out for the evening...as Stacie had asked me to do...I think she was sending him a message that he didn't like."[7]

When Stacie began dating him, Jason had seemed like a sweetheart and was adopted by the entire Madison family like some stray puppy. But as time wore on, Stacie had grown weary of not only the boy's insecurities and jealous nature but also his controlling ways. He had, according to Stacie's family, maneuvered to isolate her from her friends in order that she might devote her time exclusively to him. Only recently Stacie had decided it was past time to end the relationship but Ida recalls that Stacie just "couldn't figure out how to break it off."[8]

Upon hearing that Stacie was planning to dump Jason, Ida had quietly jumped for joy, as she had come to view him as a "practiced liar" and suspected that the bruises that kept mysteriously appearing on Stacie's body, such as the ones she had seen on her daughter's legs and thighs, were his doing.[9]

At this moment in time, though, all Ida wanted was for her daughter to come home. They could talk later on about where Stacie had been and why she had been gone so long. Right now, Ida wanted her daughter to be home, safe and sound.

The clock continued to tick away the hours. Sunday night became Monday morning, and Ida found herself unable to sleep. So, she sat down in a chair situated in front of one of the living room's front windows and kept vigil there until sunrise.

---

6 Please note that "Jason Lawton" is not this individual's true name.

7 Ida Madison, June 20, 2009.

8 *The Dallas Morning News*, August 19, 2001.

9 Ida Madison, June 20, 2009.

3

MONDAY, MARCH 21, 1988

Certain now that something was deeply amiss…

Early the next morning, Monday, March 21, 1988, an exhausted yet frantic Frank and Ida Madison sat down and discussed their options.

Knowing Stacie would recognize she was going to be in what Ida termed "big trouble" for leaving her family to wonder for more than 24 hours just where in the world she had been, Ida suggested Frank drive to Newman Smith High School to see if perhaps Stacie had bypassed the Madison household that morning and simply gone directly to school from wherever she was in order to avoid her parents' wrath.

Arriving at the school well before it opened, Frank explained the situation to the security guards on patrol.

1967 Ford Mustangs were hard to miss, even in 1967, and in 1988, they attracted attention like a spotlight. Stacie's car was no exception, and the security guards knew immediately the car that the shaken and disheveled Frank Madison was trying to describe.

The security guards, they said, could go Frank one better. They told him that, although they had not seen it that morning, without fail Stacie always parked her car in the same vicinity of the school parking lot. (Ida Madison told me that Stacie was nothing if not predictable.[1]) The guards told Frank where he should look, provided the car was even on the grounds.

Frank thanked the men and headed to the section of the parking lot to which they had directed him. Stacie's car was not there.

Certain now that something was deeply amiss, Frank Madison crossed Josey Lane and turned into the parking lot of the Carrollton Police Department, which was virtually across the street from the high school. Once inside the police station, he approached the officer behind the glass and found his voice cracking as he realized he was saying the eight words no parent should ever have to utter – "I need to report my daughter as missing."

---

1 Ida Madison, June 20, 2009.

Stacie Madison's 1967 Ford Mustang
(Photo courtesy of Ida Madison)

4

STACIE

We both took driver's education through Sears. I will never forget sitting in the back when it was Stacie's turn to drive and her looking at the instructor and asking, "Now this is the brake and this is the gas, right?" I giggled, thinking she was joking, but she was serious. I said a quick prayer and off we went.[1]

At the time she was reported missing, Stacie Madison was described by authorities as being five feet, six inches tall, 160 pounds, 17 years old, with blonde hair and blue eyes.

Statistically, this was all true, as was the fact that, with a birthday of June 17, 1970, Stacie was the eldest of three girls born to Frank and Ida Madison.

Yet, Stacie was so much more than this. She was a bright, intelligent, multi-faceted individual, who was – according to one anonymous individual – at times so "bubbly" that it was annoying.

Others remember Stacie differently, though, and it is through their recollections that Stacie's story is told.

A BEAUTIFUL PERSON BOTH INSIDE AND OUT

Stacie's best friend in life was probably Heidi Monk Wilhelm, who says:

> Stacie Elisabeth Madison was a beautiful person both inside and out. Whether it was her appearance, her schoolwork, her friends or family, Stacie took pride in all she associated herself with. Although quiet and shy at times, she had an inner confidence that exceeded most. From birth we were destined to be friends for life. Our mothers were best friends, our dads the same. Our houses were a mere five steps away from each other. As children we spent almost every day together. From family vacations to hours upon hours on the phone with each other, we learned and experienced a lot with one another.[2]

---

1 Heidi Monk Wilhelm, September 24, 1009.
2 Id.

Stacie Elisabeth Madison
(Photo courtesy of Ida Madison)

THIS NIGHT WOUNDS TIME

A DADDY'S GIRL

"Stacie was my very first friend," said Stacey Allmon Simpson. "She lived across the street when we were little. I used to go to Bluebirds at her house. She was so close to her Dad."[3]

There is no question that Stacie was definitely a "Daddy's Girl." All those who knew both father and daughter make this point. "They had that special bond," says Ida Madison, "that I think all Dads have for their little girls."[4] Stacie's 1967 Mustang had, in fact, been a gift from the father who doted on her.

A GIRLY GIRL

It would have been hard for Frank Madison to not be enamored with Stacie. In addition to being extremely well mannered and polite, she took great pride in being what some people refer to as a "girly girl."

Some little girls enjoy climbing trees, wrestling, playing sports and rough-housing in general. This was not Stacie Madison. Instead, she seemed to be drawn only to the most feminine of activities.

Friends and family recall a young girl who delighted in collecting panda bears and going to Sunday school at the Baptist church she attended regularly with her parents and her sisters, Sara and Stefanie. In this regard, Stacie's friend Heidi adds, "As we grew older, we focused more on shopping, wearing makeup, fixing our hair, music and slumber parties."[5] In any event, Stacie was no tomboy. This her parents learned early on, when it was determined that sports, such as soccer, were simply not for her.

A BATON TWIRLING CAMP FIRE GIRL

Instead, Stacie found her passion in baton twirling, an activity at which she excelled and for which she won numerous awards in the years to come.

According to Michelle Bolig Huber, who shared baton twirling classes with Stacie, "She was much better than most of us in class and a very sweet girl."[6]

Sheryl Rummans Giles was on the baton team with both Stacie and Heidi Monk Wilhelm. Giles says:

3 Stacey Allmon Simpson, March 7, 2009 and June 8, 2009.
4 "Clinging to hope: with no new leads in Carrolton teens' disappearance, parents fear worst," *The Dallas Morning News*, May 15, 1988.
5 Heidi Monk Wilhelm, September 24, 2009.
6 Michelle Bolig Huber, August 10, 2009.

Stacie Elisabeth Madison
(Photo courtesy of Ida Madison)

I always looked up to Stacie and Heidi...I remember how Stacie would never give up when learning new routines and tricks. She would practice over and over until she mastered each move. She always offered helpful advice to the younger ones of us. She would include us and open her circle for us all to feel comfortable.[7]

Perhaps the most entertaining story regarding Stacie's twirling belongs to Heidi Monk Wilhelm. Of her days of twirling with Stacie, she says:

Baton twirling was also a very big part of our lives. Many hours were spent practicing in gyms and on driveways getting ready for the next competition...we both loved baton twirling. There was one instance where I didn't love it so much and Stacie shined brightly – literally. Our coach gave us each a set of fire batons. We were both very excited. Stacie lit hers and twirled like there was no fire at all heating up the shaft of the baton. I, on the other hand, ran![8]

Michelle Rohne also twirled with Stacie and was involved with her in Camp Fire Girls. She offers, "We always bunked together at summer camp. The thing I remember most about her is her smile. She had the biggest, most infectious smile."[9]

AN INFECTUOUS SMILE

Melody Sutton Whipple agrees and says Stacie's smile would "light up any room. Her smile was so genuine; you couldn't help smiling along with her."[10]

This smile, which many people recall, often shone brightest during holidays, which the Madison family celebrated with the greatest of enthusiasm.

At Halloween, it was not uncommon for the Madisons to all dress up in costume and then go trick-or-treating as a family. It was their Christmas celebrations, though, during which they would sometimes erect as many as three Christmas trees, for which the Madisons were famous.

---

7 Sheryl Rummans Giles, September 13, 2009.
8 Heidi Monk Wilhelm, September 24, 2009.
9 Michelle Rhone, August 25, 2009.
10 Melody Sutton Whipple, September 8, 2009.

Stacie Elisabeth Madison
(Photo courtesy of Ida Madison)

A BIG SISTER

Stacie also delighted in being a big sister to the other two girls born to Frank and Ida Madison: Sara (born in 1973) and Stefanie (born in 1981).

Of her sister, Stefanie Madison, who was six years old when Stacie disappeared, told me:

> I actually have very few memories of Stacie. There are a few times I remember us hanging out around the house. Stacie was a great sister. She was always very caring and protective of me. I wish I had more memories of her, more time with her.[11]

Of course, there are moments involving Stacie that others wish they could forget.

FAULTS AND ALL

For example, recalls Heidi Monk Wilhelm, there was the time when:

> Stacie and I, at about the age of six or seven, decided it would be fun to create an ice rink of sorts on Ida's kitchen floor. We used Palmolive dish washing soap and ice cubes. I'm not sure where the idea came from. I just remember we had a blast slipping and sliding. Then Ida came home.[12]

There was also the time Stacie and Heidi first tried their hand at toilet papering a house. As Heidi remembers it:

> I remember our first experience was at, I believe, the age of nine or ten. I had spent the night with Stacie at her house and we decided it would be fun to toilet paper a house. Too scared to go far, we opted for doing her house. I remember being scared every time a car would drive by and hiding in the bushes. Needless to say, the following morning we were in a lot of trouble with Ida; one for sneaking out; the other for wasting the toilet paper. We spent that morning cleaning it up and I think the next week apart from one another.[13]

---

11 Stefanie Madison, September 8, 2009.
12 Heidi Monk Wilhelm, September 24, 2009.
13 Id.

20

Stacie Elisabeth Madison in her beloved
"American Business Women's Competition" sweatshirt
(Photo courtesy of Ida Madison)

Then there was Stacie's determination to keep her father, a telephone company employee, in business. Says Heidi:

> We spent hours on the phone. To this day, I still do not know what we found to talk about for the amount of time we spent on the phone. We saw each other every day. Our moms had a rule, though, off by 10:00 p.m., which, of course, many times was pushed past the limit.[14]

When Stacie was not enjoying the company of her family, twirling, toilet papering houses, or talking on the phone, she was dancing.

A DANCER

It was via this avenue that Amy Cloninger Schomerus met a 12 year old Stacie:

> I was in Wranglers with Stacie when we were just kids…Wranglers was a drill team back in the late 1970s and early 1980s. Stacie was a drum major, and I was in her drum line. She was always so nice and kind of shy, but she always made you feel welcome.

In Schomerus' opinion, Stacie was "just a really sweet girl."[15]

A NEAT FREAK, BUT NO SAINT

"Sweet" and "shy" are how many remember Stacie Madison. Some, though, describe her as a "neat freak determined to have a tidy room," whose "bed and bathroom were always in order" and who would often "clean the house without being asked."[16] "She was very good at helping me out and did keep her room immaculate," says Ida Madison.[17] However, Ida makes the points that, "Stacie wasn't a saint….as her mother, there were times she wasn't quite so perfect." Instead, Ida admits, "At times I could have rung her neck and didn't. We'd just have a nice little chat.[18]

---

14 Id.
15 Amy Cloninger Schomerus, March 23, 2009 and August 11, 2009.
16 *The Fort Worth Star-Telegram*, March 18, 1998.
17 Ida Madison, September 8, 2009.
18 Id.

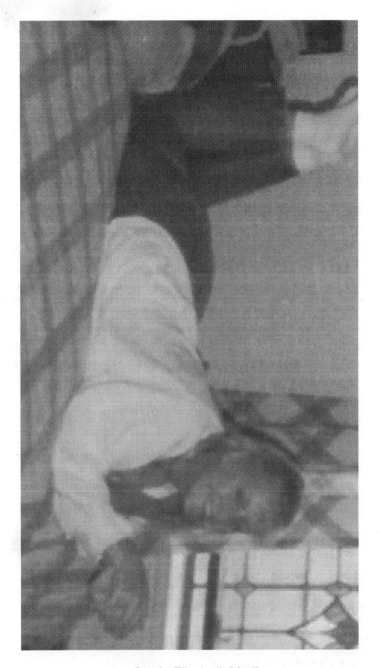

Stacie Elisabeth Madison
(Photo courtesy of Ida Madison)

As is often the case with mothers and daughters, these "nice little chats" increased in frequency as Stacie grew older.

A BAND NERD

As she entered high school, while focusing on making good grades, Stacie decided to limit her extracurricular activities to baton twirling and playing in the band.

Although her individual musical tastes ran in the direction of Air Supply, Journey, the soundtrack for the movie *Xanadu*, and the song "We Built This City on Rock and Roll" by Starship, Stacie's assigned instrument was the French horn.

Of Stacie's days in band, Jon Bohls, the Head Band Director at Smith from 1979 until 1988, recalls:

> I just remember a vibrant and bubbly girl that always seemed to be in a good mood. She was not the best horn player, but you knew that she was always working hard to do what I wanted. Her disposition was always something that you could count on to make the situation feel relaxed, even if it was getting a little tense...she blended in and was quiet in the class setting. She never was going to be a discipline problem. She paid attention and was ready to do when it was time. But I saw her being "loud" when she was around her set of friends. So she had both sides in her, which is typical.[19]

Jon Bohls was not the only faculty member to be impressed by Stacie.

A REALLY GOOD KID

When Stacie and Susan disappeared in March of 1988, Karen Lewis, the girl's vocational education teacher stated to *The Dallas Morning News*, "They're both very dependable and have had good attendance at school. Their employers always have good things to say about them. This [disappearance] is very unusual for them."[20] Sheryl Lackey, a counselor at Smith, would say, "They're both basically A and B students. They are above average."[21]

These traits were not lost on students.

---

19 Jon Bohls, July 17, 2009.
20 Kathy Jackson, "'This is just a heart-rending situation,'" *The Dallas Morning News*, March 25, 1988.
21 Id.

Stacie Elisabeth Madison
(Photo courtesy of Ida Madison)

Shannon Moller, who knew the two girls, described both to me as "really good kids" who made "really good grades."[22]

This is evidenced by the inclusion of their names on the Smith honor roll numerous times.

It is also proven by the recollections of people such as Laura Glaser, who said, "I do remember Stacy from high school. She generously let me copy off her math homework, often. She was much better at geometry than I was."[23]

A PRETTY BLONDE

Stacie also captured attention for another reason: she had grown into a very pretty girl with unavoidable blue eyes and a pile of blonde hair.

In Texas, there's the saying, "The bigger the hair, the closer to God," and there were times when those who knew Stacie thought perhaps she took this statement literally.

"Stacie was the one we called 'Miss America,'" Ida Madison told me. "We'd get ready to go someplace. We'd all four be ready, but Stacie was still in the bathroom getting her hair just so and getting her makeup just so."[24]

According to Ida Madison, Stacie had actually stopped going to Camp Fire Girls Camp a couple of years earlier because there was no electricity there, which meant she would have been unable to plug in her precious hot rollers.

A VERY SWEET GIRL

All humor aside, Stacie's meticulousness paid off, and the boys at school began to notice the girl whose outward appearance came to match her inner beauty.

Among them was Greg Batchelor, who told me:

> I met Stacie at a high school football game. I was a sophomore. She was a freshman in the band. We talked, and a relationship grew from there. We spent all of our time together. I would go out with her and her family, and vice

---

22 Shannon Moller, July 8, 2009.
23 Laura Glaser, February 7, 2009.
24 Ida Madison, June 20, 2009.

Stacie Elisabeth Madison
(Photo courtesy of Ida Madison)

versa. This lasted, as a serious relationship, for about one year. I remember how much she meant to me and me to her.[25]

However, as often happens with high school sweethearts, Stacie and Batchelor found themselves wearing on one another's nerves from time to time and sporadically taking breaks from one another. This happened once too often, and the break became permanent. After her final split with Greg Batchelor, Stacie wound up dating Jason Lawton whom she met while working part-time after school at the McDonald's restaurant near her parents' home.

AN ANGEL OF MERCY

Despite this relationship with Lawton, some of her friends speculate that Stacie may have still had feelings for Batchelor. True or not, she unquestionably never stopped caring about her old flame. In the spring of 1985, Batchelor was hospitalized with a collapsed lung. His recollection of this event is that, despite their break-up:

> The first person to visit me was Stacie. She visited frequently and, when not there, she would call me. I stayed in the hospital for 30 days, 11 of which were in ICU. The entire time, Stacie was the one person who was there for me. This was while we were not together and had not even really talked much prior to my entering the hospital.

Batchelor says, "Stacie was very sweet, and did just about anything for anyone."[26] Ida Madison agrees and says, "She was very compassionate."[27]

Of Stacie and of his hospitalization, Batchelor says:

> Stacie was my first true love of my teenage years. This is the time that I remember most. I wish I could go back and relive it again, even with the seriousness of my medical problems. I was in College Station the weekend Stacie disappeared, and when I heard the news, the way she looked after me during that time in my life was my first thought.[28]

---

25 Greg Batchelor, August 19, 2009.
26 Id.
27 Ida Madison, June 20, 2009.
28 Greg Batchelor, August 19, 2009.

Stacie Elisabeth Madison
(Photo courtesy of Ida Madison)

Whether her actions were sparked by unresolved feelings for Batchelor or not, Stacie was dating Jason Lawton at the time. And that was that.

A LONG-SUFFERING GIRLFRIEND

Stacie's decision to date Jason Lawton was one she would apparently come to regret. According to more than one source, Lawton was an insecure and jealous boyfriend with an intensely possessive streak and a quick temper. These truths first came to Ida's attention when bruises began mysteriously appearing on Stacie's body. When queried by her mother, Stacie explained them away as being the result of some rough housing in which she had engaged with Lawton. Ida, however, was skeptical of this explanation.[29]

IN ISOLATION

During Stacie's junior year in high school, says Ida, Lawton insisted that Stacie give up baton twirling.[30] Lawton declared that his intent for making this demand was that he wanted Stacie to be able to spend more time with him. Ida and others, though, believe Lawton simply wanted to distance Stacie from her friends on the twirling team.[31]

When I spoke with him during the course of writing this book, Lawton claimed this allegation is ridiculous since he and Stacie were "off and on" so often during that period and always "by Stacie's doing."[32]

Lawton also asserted that it was during this period that Stacie began "hanging around with people she hadn't been hanging around with before."[33] This, however, is not particularly surprising since, whether it was Lawton's goal or not, Stacie's resignation from the twirling team did create an unintentional divide between she and her friends.

Perhaps it was nothing calculated, but rather the sort of estrangement that occurs when one gives up a particular activity.

As Heidi Monk Wilhelm puts it:

> The normal stress of high school and other outside influences kept us from seeing each other as much during our last year of high school. But when we were together, we were one. We

29 Ida Madison, June 20, 2009.
30 *The Dallas Morning News*, August 19, 2001.
31 Ida Madison, June 20, 2009.
32 Jason Lawton, July 15, 2009.
33 Id.

knew each other's strengths and weaknesses. The bond we had formed was unbreakable. We knew one would always be there for the other.[34]

Stacie's circle of friends diminished further still during the first semester of her senior year, as she became involved in Smith's vocational education program.

Quite simply, Stacie did not have the time to work the job she had taken in the office of allergist Dr. Jeffrey Adelglass, make good grades and continue playing the French horn in the band. So, as had been the case with twirling, band fell by the wayside with a thud.

No longer involved with band or the twirling team, Stacie suddenly discovered that, at least when not in school or at work, she actually had free time with which she could do as she pleased.

Still loving to shop, as most high school girls do, and finding her band and twirling friends still engaged in those activities, it is not particularly surprising that Stacie would seek out new friends. Nor is it remarkable that she found a kindred spirit in a girl whom she met in her vocational education class – a girl whose story was somewhat similar to Stacie's own.

This girl too had recently made some radical changes in her life. She had given up athletics, namely basketball, in order to work two jobs so that she could save up enough money to buy a new car. As a result, she was also missing her longtime friends. Her name was Susan Smalley.

34 Heidi Monk Wilhelm, September 24, 2009.

5

SAPP AND BOCK

"An open missing person case doesn't carry the
same urgency as an open homicide investigation."

When the girls were reported missing in March 1988, the case –
which was and still is classified as a "missing persons" case – was first
assigned to investigators Ohlen L. Sapp and David W. Bock of the
Carrollton Police Department's Juvenile Section.

"Ohlen was the lead investigator," David Bock told me. "I assisted
at the start of the case."[1]

The case had fallen to Sapp and Bock for two reasons: Stacie
Madison and Susan Smalley were both students at Newman Smith
High School in Carrollton, Texas, which technically made them
juveniles in the eyes of the city, even though Susan Smalley was
legally an adult; and the Juvenile Section was the unit tasked with
handling all missing persons cases.

RELATIVELY INEXPERIENCED

At that time, Mr. Sapp and Mr. Bock were both young men in their
late 20s. They had each been with the Carrollton Police Department
for approximately four years, but both had held the rank of investigator
for less than one year.

Bock recalled, when I was finally able to interview him in October
2009, "It was just [Ohlen] and I in Juvenile...Juvenile is kind of where
[the Carrollton Police Department brought] you in to start. So, we
were not experienced investigators at that time."[2]

OVERWORKED AND UNDERSTAFFED

In addition to their relative inexperience, the two men say they
lacked much in the way of support from the Carrollton Police
Department.

Momentarily reinserting himself into the landscape of March 1988,
Bock remembered:

---

1 David W. Bock, September 21, 2009.
2 Id., October 17, 2009.

This is a missing persons case, so it drops to Ohlen and I. We're the only two working it...the department gave us overtime but, other than that, I don't believe they gave us any support...we didn't get any other manpower support...and, again, here we have less than a year on as investigators.[3]

Their challenges would be further compounded by another factor beyond their control – the categorization of the case.

SEMANTICS – HOMICIDE VERSUS MISSING PERSONS

Since there was initially a certain amount of skepticism regarding whether something had happened to the girls or whether they had run away, the Madison/Smalley case was classified as a missing persons case. In this regard, Ohlen Sapp offered:

[The case] did come to us as a missing person case. There was no sign or indication from the information we had initially that there'd been any foul play or anything like that. We did have Spring Break going on at the time and there was a prevailing thought that [Stacie and Susan] went to Padre or whatever.[4]

The case, as previously noted, remains a missing persons case in 2009.[5] The Carrollton Police Department's rationale for classifying it as such, both initially and currently, is understandable since to classify otherwise would mean removing the girls from the nationwide database of missing persons against which remains are matched.

At the same time, it is also regrettable since this decision has defined the department's handling of the case in a number of ways. As David Bock says, "A missing person case is approached much differently than a homicide."[6] Specifically, he says, "An open missing person case doesn't carry the same urgency as an open homicide investigation."[7] By the time I was able to interview Mr. Sapp and Mr. Bock, this was a truth I understood all too well. By that time, I had already been pursuing the Madison/Smalley case for six months and had already been privy to the insights of two other investigators in the case.

---

3 Id.
4 Ohlen Sapp, October 17, 2009.
5 John W. Crawford, October 20, 2009.
6 David Bock, October 17, 2009.
7 Id., September 22, 2009.

6

EVERYBODY TURNS OUT FINE

"It's a very rare occurrence when a person...completely disappears."

Anyone who watches police dramas on television has witnessed the formulaic scenes in which a frantic parent is told by a grizzled and weary police detective that one must wait anywhere between 24 and 72 hours before reporting an individual as missing. Such regulations are largely the product of television tradition and, in reality, do not exist.

In actuality, one may report someone missing at any time, and people are admonished to do so immediately in cases involving missing minors. It must be noted, however, that missing persons cases involving adults, particularly ones in which there is no evidence of foul play, are not afforded the same sense of urgency by police as are cases involving minor children. In instances where an adult is reported missing by a concerned relative, police sometimes do little more initially than indulge them by formalizing a report.

These truths I learned on a miserably hot afternoon when I took a day off from work to go speak with the Carrollton Police Department regarding the Madison and Smalley disappearances.

NORTH BY NORTHWEST?

It was Thursday, June 4, 2009, and I was scheduled to meet with Sergeant John W. Crawford. An officer with the Carrollton Police Department since 1990, Crawford was the supervisor of the Carrollton Police Department's Crimes Against Persons Section at the time that I spoke with him.

Since the days of Sapp and Bock in 1988, the Madison/Smalley case has changed hands numerous times in the past two decades. Among those entrusted with it over the years had been officers Greg Ward, Gary Fernandez and Glen Michna. Sergeant Crawford had never worked the case to the extent that Sapp, Bock or Ward had. Nevertheless, there was no question he would be able to provide insights into the Carrollton Police Department's handling of the case that I was eager to hear.

34

I was anxious about the interview, so I wound up arriving far too early and spent nearly half an hour in my car listening to the radio while cranking the air conditioner.

My apprehension regarding this interview with Sergeant Crawford stemmed from my trepidation about what the man might make of my desire to meet with him in order to discuss this case.

Just days after receiving the green light from the Madison and Smalley families, I learned that one of Stacie Madison's high school friends was making inquiries about me in an effort to determine just how altruistic my motives really were. What if the police turned out to be just as suspicious of me as this person?

I had, after all, been in town the week that the girls disappeared in March 1988, and I was now waiting to milk the police department for as many details about the case as they would provide.

Profilers say perpetrators of crimes oftentimes try to ingratiate themselves into police investigations so as to derive some secondary thrill from learning additional information about their victims. What if, like a page from some twisted Franz Kafka novel, the police got some wild notion that I was the mystery man they had been hunting these past 21 years?

I was familiar with those Alfred Hitchcock movies wherein some poor sap finds himself wrongfully accused of an offense he did not commit and then spends the next 90 minutes running here and there, dodging crop dusters, stealing cars, siphoning gas tanks, and climbing on the face of Mount Rushmore all before authorities realize in the last five minutes of the movie that he was not the man they were seeking in the first place.

One thing was certain; I was too old and out of shape to spend any amount of time doing anything as creative and daring as all that. I would soon discover that these anxieties were unnecessary.

THE MISSING POSTER AGAIN

As 2:00 p.m. edged ever closer, I turned off my car and ventured inside the stationhouse of the Carrollton Police Department.

There, after announcing my purpose to a uniformed officer behind a glass window, I busied myself with looking at the various keepsakes from Carrollton's past (yellowed newspaper clippings, retired service revolvers, badges and sleeve patches) stored safely inside of glass display cases.

Upon hearing a door open, and presuming it might be Sergeant Crawford, I glanced to my left and spied a bulletin board on which something was tacked that I had overlooked prior to that moment. There, on the police station's wall, was a missing poster of Stacie

Madison and Susan Smalley identical to the one I had stared at in stunned silence 21 years before.

I literally gasped in surprise as the reality sank in that this poster had most likely been hanging in this same spot that entire time - 21 years without answers or resolution.

I tried to imagine in that moment what it was like for the Madison and Smalley families and could not, as that is a reality that can only be understood by one who has lived it. The sight sent a chill down my spine despite the day's heat, and I was grateful to have the door open once more and to finally hear my name called.

JOHN W. CRAWFORD

Sergeant Crawford turned out to be a linebacker of a man with closely cropped hair. I guessed him to be about five years younger than myself. He ushered me into his office and, following some polite small talk about a variety of local topics, we got down to business.

RUNAWAYS?

Months after I interviewed Sergeant Crawford, David Bock would tell me, "The investigation never indicated the girls were runaways."[1]

However, in 2001, a later investigator on the case was quoted by *The Dallas Morning News* as saying that someone in the Carrollton Police Department had originally believed the girls were runaways.[2]

Therefore, my first question for Sergeant Crawford concerned why, in the initial hours following Frank Madison's report that his daughter was missing, the Carrollton Police Department had been so seemingly slow to respond and why police had apparently presumed both girls had run away.

I anticipated his response would involve the words "Spring Break" and that there existed the strong likelihood that the girls were just skipping school and taking an extra day off.

Sergeant Crawford's answer, though, could not have been more removed from such reasoning, and frankly it caught me by surprise.

A COMMON OCCURRENCE

When it came to cases involving missing adults, he said, in at least "98% of them, everybody turns out fine," and, as a result, seasoned police officers operate from a vantage point wherein the standard

---

1 Id.
2 *The Dallas Morning News*, August 19, 2001.

presumption is, "Hopefully, we're going to get a good resolution to this, but you don't know."[3]

With just these few words, Sergeant Crawford shattered the myth television creates of the police officer ready to spring into action at the slightest mention of a disappearance. His words also made me realize police officers do not think like everyday people in that they do not make snap judgments. They are trained not to do so. This is what empowers them to perform the tasks they are entrusted to do.

As well, veteran police officers learn to avoid joining families in their anxieties over missing persons. To do so would hinder their abilities to think rationally in moments when others are panicking. Moreover, as Sergeant Crawford pointed out, in nearly all the missing persons cases the Carrollton Police Department has dealt with over the years, "Where people have sworn somebody's been killed, they usually fall off the wagon and go back into alcohol or substance abuse when they come up missing." Until that moment, I had not considered that the police did not view the girls as children or even as minors. Instead, although it was being handled by the Juvenile Section, as far as the department was concerned, the girls were two adults whose whereabouts were currently unknown.

I had also not considered just how commonplace missing persons, including minors, are. Sergeant Crawford's next statement, though, made avoiding that truth impossible. "At any one time," he said, "we'll have a dozen runaways or missing persons. Every day or two," he continued, "we get some Mom or Dad calling in with 'My kid is missing' and 99.5% of them are located within a few days." Moreover, in most cases involving missing adults, the sergeant revealed, the person has "gone off to a friend's and ends up coming home...it's a very rare occurrence when a person, much less two people, completely disappears."[4]

MELANIE GOODWIN

Readers should not presume, based upon his matter of fact approach, that the sergeant is a calloused or unfeeling individual. In fact, I would say the opposite is true. In interviewing him, I learned he had been one of a team of investigators that had helped capture Ernesto Reyes, the man who, in September 2007, had inexplicably raped, murdered and then burned University of North Texas student and model Melanie Goodwin. That tragic incident – which Crawford mentioned multiple times in order to illustrate how both standard investigative procedures and the manner in which security camera

---

3 John W. Crawford, June 4, 2009.
4 Id.

footage has improved since 1988 – had obviously affected the sergeant deeply.

PERSPECTIVE

After speaking with Sergeant Crawford, I could see the police department's side of things. On a purely conceptual level, I understood why police had not released the bloodhounds at the first hint that something was amiss. That is not to say, though, that I – as I am sure police do too – do not wish things had been handled differently.

Another person who wishes things had been handled differently is Susan's father, John Richard Smalley, who insists that police sat on their hands for too long and did not take the case seriously until the local media began pressuring them for answers. Until they decided to act, he says, the Madison and Smalley families had no recourse but to wait and wonder about their loved ones and about what the police intended to do about the situation.[5]

Carolyn Smalley, however, disputes this and insists:

> I never felt like the police didn't take it seriously. I never had that feeling. Maybe that first day when I went in there and reported it, but when I talked to them the next day afterward, and Stacie and Susan still weren't home, I think the police realized they were good girls.[6]

So, did the police take an inexplicably lengthy amount of time to spring into action? Did they not take the case seriously enough initially? Unfortunately, there are no easy answers to these questions.

I do know that Ohlen Sapp would eventually tell me, "The City of Carrollton and us [David Bock and Ohlen Sapp] did the best that we could with what we had to work with at the time," and I saw nothing but sincerity on his face at the moment that these words were uttered.[7] I believe Mr. Sapp was telling me the truth.

I know that not everyone shares my opinion.

I must, therefore, since so much in this regard is dependent upon one's perspective, leave it to the readers to be the final arbiters of these difficult questions.

---

5 Id.
6 Carolyn Smalley, July 14, 2009.
7 Ohlen Sapp, October 17, 2009.

7

THE FORD MUSTANG

The car's convertible top had been secured and the doors were locked. The girls' purses, though, were nowhere to be found.

Ida Madison literally spent the entirety of Tuesday, March 22, 1988 on the telephone, first exchanging calls with family and friends in the hopes that someone had seen Stacie and Susan, and then calling the police to see if they had learned anything new. She would then begin the cycle of calls anew. A "take charge" personality, Ida could not sit still, not while her daughter was missing. She had to do something, so she invariably found the telephone in her hand, as she dialed one number and then another. Surely, she thought, there was a logical explanation for all of this. Someone had to know something.

Frank Madison too was not content to just sit around and wait.

The previous day, on Monday, March 21, 1988, he and Jason Lawton, Stacie's boyfriend, had formed a scouting party and, traversing the Dallas roadways, had ventured to every conceivable place to which Stacie and Susan might have gone.

When I queried Lawton about his and Frank's efforts that day, Lawton told me, "Frank called and wanted to go look. I really don't remember where we went. I didn't put too much effort in it." Lawton does seem to recall, though, that they explored the area surrounding Lake Lewisville.

Ida recalls Frank mentioning that at some point in the afternoon he and Jason had driven down Forest Lane, the premier cruise spot for North Dallas teenagers. When I asked him about this, Lawton said, "I don't think we went towards Dallas."[1]

If the two did venture down Forest Lane, they overlooked something of major importance.

THE BASEBALL CARD SHOP

On Sunday, March 20, 1988, the owner of a baseball card shop in the Webbs Chapel Village – situated within a strip center at the intersection of Webbs Chapel Road and Forest Lane – noticed a late

---

1 Jason Lawton, July 15, 2009.

1960s Ford Mustang parked in front of his place of business. He thought nothing of this since a friend of his drove a Mustang similar to the one at which he was now looking. His presumption was that the friend had merely parked the car, gone somewhere for the day, and would retrieve it later.

The car sat in the parking lot for the entirety of Sunday.

THE CARD SHOP OWNER

The next morning, Monday, March 21, 1988, the card shop owner arrived at work and was irritated to discover the car still parked in front of his business. Leaving a car unattended for one day was one thing, and maybe allowing it to sit there overnight was even acceptable. The car, though, had now been sitting there for at least 24 hours and that was just plain uncool. The card shop owner attempted to call his friend on the telephone but got no answer. He would have to call back later.

THE FRIEND

The two men finally connected that afternoon, and the shop owner was quick to remind his friend that, in case he had forgotten, his Mustang was taking up one of his prime parking spots, and it was in his friend's best interest to come and get it.

"I don't know what you're talking about, man! My car's right here," the friend said.

After apologizing to his friend for being so presumptuous, the card shop owner chatted with the man for a few more minutes, particularly about the oddity of the situation, before hanging up.

That was for sure weird, the shop owner thought.

If that was not his friend's car, then to whom did it belong and how had it come to be in this parking lot?

THE CONNECTION MADE

As the afternoon wore on, the card shop owner simply could not stand it any longer. That Mustang had now been in the parking lot since at least Sunday morning, and he was beginning to fear someone had dumped a stolen car square in front of his livelihood. Picking up the telephone, he dialed the strip center's security office.

By the next day, Tuesday, March 22, 1988, Carrollton police were on the scene to examine the car, which had been listed as a stolen vehicle.

The parking lot at Webbs Chapel Road and Forest Lane
in which Stacie Madison's 1967 Ford Mustang was located
(Photo by the author)

Police noted Stacie Madison's portable stereo boom box was hidden in the floorboard of the car's back seat beneath two jackets which Susan and Stacie had borrowed from Carolyn Smalley's closet on Saturday night. The car's convertible top had been secured and the doors were locked. The girls' purses, though, were nowhere to be found.[2] In fact, according to Ida, police:

> ...have never found any sign of either girls' purse nor of any of the things in the purses. Stacie's driver's license expired, and her Social Security Number was not used. Police checked that every spring to see if anyone filed under her number.[3]

WHAT COULD IT MEAN - THE MADISONS

Upon learning of its discovery, Frank and Ida Madison found themselves going back and forth regarding what it meant that Stacie's car had been located.

One minute they found themselves hopeful, thinking that perhaps its discovery meant Stacie and Susan had simply gone off with friends and would soon return. The next moment, they believed it evidenced their worst fears.

Stacie had mentioned earlier in the month that it would be fun to go to South Padre Island for Spring Break, but she had also quickly realized she did not have the money required for such a trip. Besides, Spring Break was now over and Stacie and Susan, both honors students, would neither one jeopardize their graduations for the sake of a few days on the beach when graduation was just a little more than two months away.

WHAT COULD IT MEAN – THE SMALLEYS

At the Smalleys' home, Carolyn Smalley found herself on an emotional rollercoaster identical to the one the Madisons were riding, as she too tried to make sense of what was happening.

In 2001, Carolyn would tell *The Dallas Morning News*:

> When I came home [on Sunday morning, March 20, 1988, Stacie and Susan] weren't home, but I wasn't alarmed...When I got up the next morning, I was surprised to notice that the living room light was still on. I always left it on for Susan if she

---

2 Ida Madison, August 12, 2009.
3 Id.

The parking lot at Webbs Chapel Road and Forest Lane
in which Stacie Madison's 1967 Ford Mustang was located
(Photo by the author)

was out for the evening. So I checked on the girls and was surprised to find Susan's bedroom empty.[4]

Originally, although she later realized the girls had not come home, Carolyn believed Susan and Stacie had simply gone on a day trip on Sunday and that they would be home soon enough. Carolyn said to me:

> Those first few days, I kept thinking, "She's going to come through that door. She's okay. Everything's alright." I just felt in my heart that everything and Susan was okay.[5]

During the daylight hours on Sunday, it had been easy to believe the girls were alright and would be returning safe and sound. But Sunday had blossomed into Monday and then Tuesday had arrived. It was growing ever more difficult to remain positive.

Carolyn would later describe her daughter with the words, "Susan never was one to go along with a crowd. She has always been an individual...I knew she'd do the right thing."[6]

Susan, like Stacie, was an honors student. She was also a go-getter who worked two jobs, was saving money to buy a car, and had plans for college. Susan, thought Mrs. Smalley, simply would not start behaving so irresponsibly at this late date.

"It's not like her (Susan)," Carolyn would say in the days immediately following her daughter's disappearance, "She's never done anything like this before."[7]

Carolyn, also acting on instinct, had reported Susan missing on Monday, March 21, 1988, when she received word from Newman Smith High School that the girls had not reported to class that morning.[8]

Now, she joined the Madisons in that cruel taunt which parents of a missing child come to despise – waiting.

4 *The Dallas Morning News*, August 19, 2001.
5 Carolyn Smalley, July 14, 2009.
6 Kathy Jackson, "Moms cling to hope for 2 missing teens," *The Dallas Morning News*, March 30, 1988.
7 Tracy Everback, "Carrollton police ask for help in finding 2 missing teen-agers," *The Dallas Morning News*, March 24, 1988.
8 Carolyn Smalley, July 14, 2009.

Susan Renee Smalley circa 1973
(Photo courtesy of Rich Smalley)

8

SUSAN

"Susan was an 'old soul' even in 8th Grade –
responsible, witty and thoughtful."[1]

Susan Renee Smalley.

Born September 19, 1969, in Dallas County, Texas, to John Richard Smalley, a firefighter with the Farmers Branch Fire Department, and Carolyn Lloyd Smalley, an insurance administrator.

Younger sister to John Richard Smalley II.

5'8" at the time of her disappearance and 140 pounds.

Brown hair, green eyes.

Honor student.

These are the particulars concerning the girl who, along with Stacie Madison, disappeared in the early morning hours of Sunday, March 20, 1988.

Yet, as with Stacie Madison, to present Susan Smalley in such narrow terms would be to diminish not only her individuality, but her significance in the lives of others and the love she possessed for those close to her.

The following, therefore, is my attempt to paint a portrait of Susan that reaches beyond mere data and statistics.

THE PHOTO ALBUM

Susan Smalley's parents were married in 1966, the same year in which Susan's brother Rich was born.

Ten years later, in 1976, the Smalleys' marriage ended in divorce.

Susan was seven years old.

During the decade he was married to the mother of his children, John Richard Smalley kept a photo album measuring at least three inches thick which chronicled the life and times of his family. While in the initial research phase of this book, I requested photos of Susan from her brother, Rich. During one of the occasions on which I met with him, Rich stunned me by graciously loaning me the photo album

---

1 Susannah Webb Rouse, October 3, 2009.

Susan Renee Smalley
(Photo courtesy of Marilyn Hutchison)

compiled by his father. For a writer reaching to become intimate with the personality of someone he never knew, this was an unimaginable gift. This pictorial history spoke, without words, volumes about the events that shaped the person Susan Smalley became.

TWEETY BIRD

Susan's aunt, Marilyn Hutchison, told me, "Susan was born two days after my birthday. I can remember hoping she would be born on my birthday."[2] Upon hearing these words, my mind recalled that among the first photos in the Smalley family album were those of an infant girl with a huge, toothless smile, enormous round eyes and a virtually hairless head.

When mentioning these photos to Carolyn Smalley, she told me that, during this period in her daughter's life, one of Susan's uncles had spied in his niece a resemblance to a beloved *Looney Tunes* character. Consequently, among certain family members, Susan was known for a time as "Tweety Bird."

JUMPERS WITH LARGE COLLARS

The nickname did not stick, as Susan grew quickly into a cute little girl with teeth that were slightly bucked, a mop of strawberry blonde hair, and a penchant for multi-colored jumpers with large collars.

This is evidenced by the Smalley's photo album, as is the undeniable truth that Susan was a little girl who was into everything.

On one page of photos, she attempts to strum an oversized guitar. On another, she and her brother Rich wrestle on the carpet. She wades in swimming pools, performs at dance recitals, smiles at birthdays, searches for eggs at Easter, squirms through a kindergarten graduation, and delights at Christmases.

One set of yuletide photos illustrates her varied interests and reflect a Christmas on which she received both a Lite Brite set and a Dressy Bessie doll.

A GOOD KID BUT HEADSTRONG

Of this period in Susan's life, her father offered only that, "She was a good kid, but headstrong."[3]

---

2 Marilyn Hutchison, September 21, 2009.
3 John Richards Smalley, July 5, 2009.

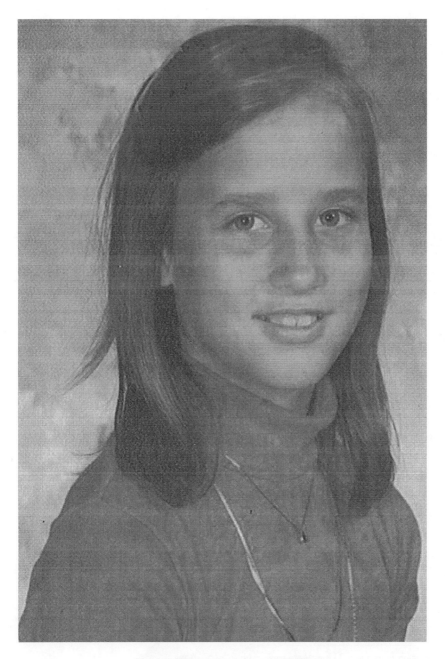

Susan Renee Smalley in 1980
(Photo courtesy of Marilyn Hutchison)

ALL OUT WAR BETWEEN SIBLINGS

Susan's brother, Rich, also remembers these days and laughingly says, "Susan was kind of a tomboy when young, eventually growing into a young lady. We got along for the most part, but there was always a chance an argument would heat up at any minute – the brother/sister thing...we'd get into fights, and she'd finally throw something or kick me or something. Then, she'd run to her room and lock herself in there. It was all out war back then."[4]

PEACE BETWEEN SIBLINGS

As is often the case with brothers and sisters, the "all out war" mellowed as time went on and, over the years, the two siblings became good friends and playmates.

"She played soccer for a while when young," Rich Smalley told me. "I remember her and I playing football or soccer in the yard when we were young. We would also play many a board game when young."

Rich also said:

> I remember her and I spending summers at our Dad's house in Dallas and then later in Odessa. We would usually do all kinds of chores during the day and do lots of playing as well. We would play with our cousins as well when at Dad's. The part of the summers we were at my Mom's, the day would usually be filled with TV and playing with neighborhood friends.[5]

Susan would never lack for friends. On this point, Rich said:

> Susan would often hang out with my friends and I when she was younger until she grew and met more friends that were girls in the neighborhood. As I got older, especially old enough to drive, I was away with friends, and she started coming into her own and meeting lots of new girlfriends in junior high and high school and forming more of her own identity besides 'Richard Smalley's little sister.'[6]

One of the ways in which Susan would form her own identity and find new friends was through her involvement in sports.

---

4 Rich Smalley, July 14, 2009 and September 20, 2009.
5 Rich Smalley, September 20, 1988.
6 Id.

Susan Renee Smalley in 1983
(Photo courtesy of Marilyn Hutchison)

A NATURAL ATHLETE

One of Susan's friends was Shannon Moller. She recalls Susan as a natural athlete with an enviable talent that transcended all sports.

By the time she entered junior high, though, Susan had decided she was best suited for volleyball, basketball and track. These three sports Susan pursued with a passion.

It was via junior high athletics that Susan also met Crystal Rainwater-Roberson, who would become not only Susan's teammate but a good friend. Mrs. Roberson told me, "Susan and I both played volleyball (she was really good), basketball, and track in the 8th Grade."[7]

AN ALL-AROUND GIRL

Despite Susan's athleticism, no one should presume she was single-minded or only able to talk sports. In fact, quite the opposite is true.

"What an amazing person Susan was," said Susan's friend Deanna Bowman Sinclair, "She was a best friend to me, and I want everyone to know her greatness and what a loss we all have without her."[8]

Sinclair would also say, "Susan would help me with homework and I would get better grades because of it."[9]

Susan would always work hard to make good grades in nearly all her subjects and, when she was old enough, would pour that same discipline into the various part-time jobs she undertook.

All of her bosses would speak highly of her. One was David Hill, the manager of the Steak and Ale at which she worked, who described Susan to the media with the words, "She's just a good kid."[10]

In between all of this hustle and bustle, Susan would find time to pursue the recreational pursuits she loved, such as attending rock concerts and going to movies. Among her favorite movies, Rich Smalley told me, was "Footloose." And her favorite band was Journey, especially the song "Don't Stop Believin'." "She also liked the music of Foreigner," said Rich. "Who didn't back then?"[11]

She also liked people and was well-liked by those who knew her. Deanna Bowman Sinclair says:

---

7 Crystal Rainwater Roberson, July 6, 2009.
8 Deanna Bowman Sinclair, September 28, 2009.
9 Id., October 1, 2009.
10 *The Dallas Morning News*, March 25, 1988.
11 Rich Smalley, September 20, 2009.

Susan Renee Smalley in 1984
(Photo courtesy of Marilyn Hutchison)

Susan was perceived as quiet and reserved. A super student! She did not stand out like the popular crowd. She was a loyal friend with a kind heart. If I needed a ride somewhere, she was there. If I needed to borrow a cool shirt from her, she was happy to do it. She was an unselfish soul. She worked hard and that did not leave much time for socializing. But she always made time for a friend.[12]

HANGING OUT AND TALKING ABOUT BOYS

Crystal Rainwater-Roberson agrees and offers, "We got along really well. She was a very kind person. She was very funny."

Roberson also added, "As with most teenagers at that age, we just liked hanging out and talking about boys."[13]

Looking back on this period in her life, Roberson adds, "I was kind of shy, but Susan never had any problems meeting or talking to guys."[14] When asked to explain her statement, Roberson explained that Susan just possessed a quiet confidence that drew people to her.

Granted, the fact that by this time Susan had grown into a pretty young woman with impressive green eyes and wavy brown hair did not hurt anything. As her father said to me, "She was a beautiful girl."[15]

CONSERVATIVE AND RESPONSIBLE

Consequently, considering she had a great personality to match her looks, it is not surprising that Susan had any number of young men interested in dating her.

In this regard, says Deanna Bowman Sinclair, "Susan was a lot of fun, but conservative and responsible...I remember she had a boyfriend who lived off Frankford Road and Marsh Lane. We [Susan and Deanna] used to hang out there a lot and go to the pool and listen to music."[16]

Of these days, Sinclair says:

I have memories of laughter, silliness and running all over Carrollton in Susan's little brown Ford Pinto...we drove around

---

12 Deanna Bowman Sinclair, October 1, 2009.
13 Crystal Rainwater-Roberson, June 2, 2009.
14 Id.
15 John Richard Smalley, July 5, 2009.
16 Deanna Bowman Sinclair, October 1, 2009.

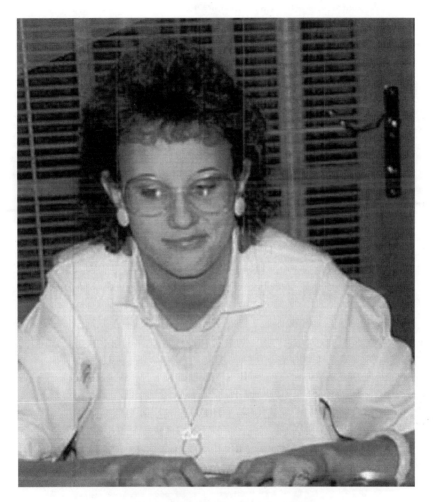

Susan Renee Smalley in 1984
(Photo courtesy of Marilyn Hutchison)

a lot. I guess you could call it "cruising," but I don't remember cruising Forest Lane that often...we would go shopping, play loud music, laugh.[17]

Of all the friends in her life during this period, though, perhaps the person closest to Susan was her mother.

KIND AND COMPASSIONATE

Susan was always close to and shared a very special bond with her mother. But beginning in 1985, said Carolyn, "When Richard left home to go to college, we [Carolyn and Susan] became even closer. We were mother and daughter and the best of friends."[18]

In this regard, Carolyn told *The Fort Worth Star-Telegram* in 2001, "We got along like sisters. She felt she could tell me anything without me being shocked or embarrassed."[19] Carolyn would also tell me, "Susan was a good kid. She was more than a daughter. She was my best friend."[20]

Consequently, says Carolyn, she came to know her daughter very well in the late 1980s. She described Susan with the following words:

> She was a very normal, happy 18 year old...her last year of school she worked two jobs, one at an office through the co-op program and the other at Steak and Ale. She made good grades and was on the honor roll...Susan was looking forward to graduation, going on a vacation with her mother to the beach, buying a new car and going to junior college for a while before she went to work full-time...she wanted more than anything to get married someday and have lots of kids. For some reason, she always wanted to have twins...she got along well with others and was a very kind and compassionate person...she and my sister were a lot alike...both would do anything to help others.[21]

These words echo what Carolyn said in 2001, when she told the *The Fort Worth Star-Telegram* that Susan was a girl who "possessed the maturity and responsibility of an older woman."[22]

---

17 Id., September 28, 2009 and October 1, 2009.
18 Carolyn Smalley, September 22, 2009.
19 *The Fort Worth Star-Telegram*, March 18, 1998.
20 Carolyn Smalley, July 14, 2009.
21 Carolyn Smalley, September 22, 2009.
22 *The Fort Worth Star-Telegram*, March 18, 1998.

Susan Renee Smalley in 1987
(Photo courtesy of Edward L. Williams)

Susan's aunt, Marilyn Hutchison, had mentioned Susan's impressive sense of responsibility to me just days earlier when recalling a conversation between herself and her sister Carolyn in the late 1980s. At that time, the two had been speculating about just who would take care of them when they were senior citizens. Marilyn remembers, "Carolyn told me that Susan would because that was the kind of caring, thoughtful young lady Susan had become. She did not shirk responsibility and would always be loyal to her family and friends."[23]

As a result, with their shared sense of devotion to family and friends, it is no surprise that Stacie Madison was drawn to the willowy brunette when they met in a vocational education class in the fall of 1987.

---

23 Marilyn Hutchison, September 21, 2009.

9

NO BLAME ON
THE CARROLLTON POLICE
DEPARTMENT

*"It's not unusual that you wouldn't 'print' a car on a
missing person case when there's no evidence of anything."*

Within hours of its discovery, Stacie Madison's Ford Mustang was
returned to the custody of her parents.

As first reported in 2001, what makes this fact controversial, at
least in hindsight, is the Carrollton Police Department's decision not to
impound the car or to check it for fingerprints prior to releasing it to
Stacie's parents.[1]

According to Ida's recollections:

> Police called us, told us where it was and to come get it. The
> police were there [Webbs Chapel Road at Forest Lane] when
> we arrived. They had popped the trunk to look for bodies, and
> told us they had processed the car. Frank realized police had
> popped the trunk after we got home, and he looked at the
> trunk. Something on the lock was bent, loose or something
> and he fixed that. Frank drove the car home from in front of
> the card shop.[2]

When I asked her if she, her husband and police discussed the
necessity of fingerprinting Stacie's car when it was discovered, Ida told
me, "My husband asked police the day the car was found whether it
had been checked for prints. Then I asked police about it again the
next morning...needless to say, it never happened."[3]

COULD HAVE HANDLED IT BETTER

For this particular decision, the Carrollton Police Department has
been repeatedly condemned.

---

1 *The Dallas Morning News*, August 19, 2001.
2 Ida Madison, October 7, 2009.
3 Id., September 18, 2009.

At times, this criticism has come courtesy of its own personnel. Case in point: Greg Ward, a later investigator on the case, was quoted in 2001 by *The Dallas Morning News* as saying that the original investigators, "[J]ust didn't process the car. They thought [the girls were runaways]. I'm not saying they screwed up, but they probably could have handled it better."[4]

"Handled it better" - those three words stayed with me.

I resolved that, if nothing else, I would pursue that particular theme further as soon as I could.

My first opportunity to ask about the fingerprinting of Stacie Madison's car (or the lack thereof) had come during my interview with Sergeant John Crawford of the Carrollton Police Department.

It was a moment we had both anticipated, but it was nevertheless a tense one.

When presented with my question, the sergeant redirected my attention to statements he had offered previously that afternoon concerning the ages of the girls, the inarguable statistic that less than 1% of all missing person cases involve foul play and the fact that almost all missing person cases result in a positive outcome.

He then expounded on these points by adding:

> It's not unusual that we get calls about someone's missing or run away, and we don't go over and 'print' a whole house and do a full crime scene every time we get one of those calls – unless there's those extenuating factors such as an eyewitness who saw some type of an abduction or there's evidence of some type of major crime there. So, again, it's not unusual when you've got somebody who says "My daughter's missing and we've found her car" [that the daughter is] with her friend…so, it's not unusual that you wouldn't 'print' a car on a missing person case when there's no evidence of anything.[5]

Once more, I could not argue with the police department's logic on an intellectual level. Still, I wanted to know more. My chance to ask additional questions came within a matter of weeks.

---

4 *The Dallas Morning News*, August 19, 2001.
5 John W. Crawford, June 4, 2009.

GREG WARD

Anyone who knows me knows I am not a morning person. So, it was almost laughable that I would schedule an interview with anyone at 7:00 a.m., let alone one at a locale 21 miles away from my home.

Yet on the appointed day, I was awake long before my alarm sounded. I had, in fact, slept little.

I was scheduled to meet that day with none other than Greg Ward – the man who had stated in 2001 that the Carrollton police could have initially "handled" the Madison/Smalley case "better."

This was a meeting I had long anticipated.

Ward has not worked for the Carrollton Police Department for a number of years but is instead employed by the Frisco Police Department, where he holds the rank of captain. Still, although not inheriting it from Sapp and Bock until the summer of 1988, Ward has the distinction of having worked the girls' case longer than any other investigator. As a result, he probably knows more about it than anyone.

My interview with him did not disappoint.

HINDSIGHT IS 20/20

As I had done with Sergeant Crawford, I began the interview with Captain Ward by reminding him that, when it comes to the Madison/Smalley case, the Carrollton Police Department stands accused in the court of public opinion of initially being both incompetent and apathetic.

In response to these comments, the captain's words echoed those of Sergeant Crawford almost verbatim.

For example, Captain Ward offered that, more often than not, cases wherein someone is abducted via foul play, "Don't happen often...less than 1%." Instead, reaffirming what Sergeant Crawford had said just weeks earlier, Ward stated, "In most runaway or missing adults cases where foul play is suspected, there is no foul play...someone just wanted to be gone."

Moreover, he reminded me that, at the time of their disappearances in 1988, Stacie Madison and Susan Smalley "were legally adults, 17 and 18 years old. They could have left and not committed an offense or a violation of the Family Code or anything like that."[6]

---

6 Greg Ward, June 16, 2009.

THE DREADED QUESTION AGAIN

Realizing that continuing this line of questioning was likely to result in further reiterations of Sergeant Crawford's previous comments, I quickly steered the conversation in the direction of Stacie's Madison's Ford Mustang and found myself posing the dreaded question about why the police had not fingerprinted the car.

"The car got released to the family before it got processed," stated the captain in a matter of fact tone.

Then, in response to my follow-up questions regarding what evidence, if any, may have been forever lost as a result of this error, he offered me his sincerest opinion:

> The car was parked. The [driver's] seat was in the normal position. I think the girls parked the car and went with somebody else. Hindsight is 20/20, but I don't think there'd have been any evidentiary value to that car...if you could do everything over, it probably wouldn't hurt, but probably all you would find is Susan's and Stacie's fingerprints all over that car. It just wasn't normal investigative procedure on missing adults...we were not treating it like a homicide.[7]

Concerning this latter statement, the reader will note that, as David Bock would note months later, "An open missing person case doesn't carry the same urgency as an open homicide investigation."[8]

OHLEN SAPP'S AND DAVID BOCK'S COMMENTS

In October 2009, I would ask Ohlen Sapp and David Bock the same questions I had posed to both John Crawford and Greg Ward regarding the reasons Stacie Madison's car was not fingerprinted. Ohlen Sapp's words were familiar to me by the time he uttered them:

> At that time [1988], Forest Lane was a hang out area. So, it wasn't unusual that the car was parked there...[and there was] absolutely no sign of a crime scene whatsoever [so fingerprinting the vehicle] wouldn't have been something, under the circumstances, in my opinion, that any investigator would have done, given the information we had at that time...had it been a different kind of investigation [e.g., a homicide investigation], oh, yeah! But it wasn't.[9]

---

7 Greg Ward, June 16, 2009.
8 David Bock, September 22, 2009.
9 Ohlen Sapp, October 17, 2009.

Echoing his former partner's words, David Bock added:

> When we responded, there was nothing unusual about the vehicle...it was parked. There was no evidence of foul play whatsoever. Obviously, whoever had parked the vehicle there went with somebody else...there was no evidence of forced entry. There was no sign of disarray, nothing. There was no reason to carry it any further. Now, knowing what we found out about three months later, it would have been nice. If you were dealing with a homicide, and you knew you were dealing with a homicide, and you found the victim's vehicle, certainly [fingerprinting the car] would have been part of the crime scene...but, at that time, again, we were dealing with missing persons who obviously locked up the car and got into another vehicle.[10]

Once more it all seemed to hinge on the fact that the case had been, and continues to be, classified as a missing persons case and not a homicide.

EVIDENCE LOST?

I would eventually relay to Ida Madison and Rich Smalley that Captain Ward's opinion was that examining the car would have most likely uncovered nothing beyond Stacie's and Susan's own fingerprints. Rich's retort was, "Of course, but it could have had something else. You never know."[11]

THE BLAME GAME

No, there is no way of knowing what secrets Stacie's car may have revealed had it been fingerprinted. So, playing Devil's Advocate, I presented this point to Captain Ward.

The emotion within his response caught me off guard.

"Society today likes to put blame on somebody," stated the captain, who quickly added, "There is no blame on the Carrollton Police Department."[12]

In that moment, I realized that, although he had never met them, here was a man who truly cared about Stacie Madison and Susan Smalley more than he could probably put into words.

---

10 David Bock, October 17, 2009.
11 Rich Smalley, June 27, 2009.
12 Greg Ward, June 16, 2009.

I glimpsed just how frustrated he was by the knowledge that, nearly 22 years after their disappearances, the mystery of March 20, 1988 remains. I also realized something else. For the past two decades, despite having its best men devote their best efforts to determining what had happened to the girls, the Carrollton Police Department has suffered in silence in the face of allegations that they dropped the ball in 1988.

Realizing this was a sore subject with Captain Ward, I quickly changed the subject to another technical point that had also given me pause.

A QUESTION OF JURISDICTION

Drawing Captain Ward's attention to the fact that Stacie Madison's car had been located in a parking lot at Webbs Chapel Road and Forest Lane, which is clearly Dallas County, I inquired as to why the Dallas Police Department had not taken control of the investigation at that point. His response let me know that his passion for the Madison/Smalley case, and his irritation at what he called the "blame game," were both still riding close to the surface:

> You can talk about who should have investigated this case...I believe in my heart Stacie and Susan were murdered, and I also believe in my heart they weren't murdered in Carrollton, Texas...for a criminal investigation, Carrollton had jurisdiction. Carrollton did the right thing. Stacie and Susan were missing from and lived in Carrollton...that's how Carrollton got involved. Sometimes the larger cities [take the attitude of] "They're adults" and "There's no evidence of foul play other than they're missing." Carrollton took the ball and ran with it.[13]

Yes, given the possibility that the Dallas Police Department might very well have done absolutely nothing about the girls' disappearances whatsoever, I could not deny that the Carrollton Police Department had recovered the ball and scrambled to get something accomplished.

God bless them for that, I thought.

THEY DID THE BEST JOB THEY COULD

As I left Captain Ward's office, I recalled Ida Madison's comments about the Carrollton Police Department's efforts to find Stacie and Susan, which included everything from flying over the Trinity River in a helicopter in the hopes of spying the girls' remains to searching both

---

13 Id.

the dumpsters behind the Webbs Chapel Village and the sewer system that ran beneath Forest Lane.

Ida told me, "This is the first and only case of this nature that the Carrollton police have ever investigated. I honestly believe they did the best job they could."[14] All things considered, I admitted she was correct in her assertion.

I was heartened by the knowledge that, although one could easily choose to emphasize the mistakes that were made, dedicated officers who took the case personally had passionately sought to solve the mystery of the girls' disappearances. Again, I thought, God bless them for that.

14 Ida Madison, August 3, 2009.

10

CARROLLTON POLICE
ASK FOR HELP

*"A $1,500 reward is being offered for
information leading to their safe return."*

As part of Newman Smith High School's Vocational Education program, Stacie Madison worked after school in the office of Dr. Jeffrey Adelglass, a prominent Metroplex allergist with ties to WFAA, the Dallas, Texas affiliate of ABC Television.

Among the WFAA employees Stacie had met via the doctor was veteran weatherman Troy Dungan who, like everyone else who met her, was struck by the 17 year old's outgoing nature and unabashed confidence.[1]

Through the doctor's friendship with Troy Dungan, the story of the disappearances of Stacie Madison and Susan Smalley finally hit the local airwaves on Wednesday, March 23, 1988, two days after Frank Madison and Carolyn Smalley had first reported their daughters as missing.

OUT OF CHARACTER

John McCaa, today one of WFAA's lead news anchors, was the one to break the story on the air during that afternoon's broadcast[2]

The following day, an expanded version of McCaa's story appeared in the *Dallas Morning News*.

"Police have issued a plea for help in finding two Carrollton high school students who have been missing since Saturday night," the story began. It continued with the details:

> Susan Renee Smalley, 18, and Stacie Elizabeth [sic] Madison, 17, both seniors at Newman Smith High School, told their parents they were going out on Saturday night and were last seen at about 1:30 a.m. Sunday by a waiter at a Steak and Ale restaurant in Addison where Miss Smalley worked...The

---

1 Ida Madison, June 20, 2009.
2 John McCaa, June 25, 2009.

young women's parents and police said they are concerned because leaving for several days without contacting their parents is out of character for Miss Smalley and Miss Madison.[3]

The article also included a curious statement about the girls' disappearances from Carrollton Police Lt. Dennis Watson, who was quoted as saying, "We're handling it like something has happened to [Stacie and Susan] but we have nothing to indicate something has."

The story provided physical descriptions of both girls: "Miss Smalley is 5-foot-8 and 140 pounds, with brown hair and green eyes" and "Miss Madison is 5-foot-6 and 160 pounds with blond hair and blue eyes."

It ended with the disclosure that a "$1,500 reward is being offered for information leading to their safe return."[4] Within a single week, the reward, offered by First Western National Bank of Carrollton, would swell to $8,500.[5] By 1989, it would stand at $10,000.[6]

The reward would not be the City of Carrollton's only gesture of care and concern for the missing girls.

---

3 *The Dallas Morning News*, March 24, 1988.
4 Id.
5 "Metro Report," *The Dallas Morning News*, March 26, 1988.
6 Bobbi Miller, "Missing students recalled," *The Dallas Morning News*, March 15, 1990.

11

THE CITY OF CARROLLTON

"A vibrant corporate and residential community…"

Carrollton, Texas is situated 14 miles north of downtown Dallas, with the North Dallas Tollway, Interstate Highway 35 and the George Bush Turnpike being the primary roadways into the city.

Consisting of 36.6 square miles, the city today is one of the more modern suburbs in the Dallas area, and has the distinction of being located in three counties – Dallas, Denton and Collin.

Nine years ago, in 2000, the population of Carrollton was at 109,576 people, with a demographic average of 6% African-American, 20% Latino, 72% Caucasian and 2% listed as "other."

At the time of the 2000 census, the median household income was $62,402, and the per capita income was $26,746.

According to the city's website, Carrollton justifiably refers to itself as:

> [A] vibrant corporate and residential community [whose] location and business cost advantages attract and support a diverse local economy. Over 5,000 businesses call Carrollton home [including] [m]anufacturing, construction trades and wholesale trades [and] finance, insurance and real estate.[1]

In 2008, *Money* magazine ranked Carrollton as "15th in the country as the Best Place to live."[2]

Things in Carrollton were not always so urbane.

THE PETERS COLONY

The first known settlers in Carrollton, Texas were William and Mary Larner, who arrived in the area in 1842. They were British immigrants who acquired land through a Peters Colony land grant. Other colonists included Thomas Keenan, Isaac Webb, and William Cochran, who, while Carrollton was being settled, were establishing a colony to the south that today is Farmers Branch, Texas.

---

http://www.cityofcarrollton.com/index.aspx?page=579.
2 Id.

SHAWN SUTHERLAND

Newman Smith
(Photo courtesy of Edward L. Williams)

THIS NIGHT WOUNDS TIME

Carrollton was officially mapped by a railway worker in 1878. At that time, just under 500 people called the city home. The original settlers of the area had been almost exclusively farmers and millers, but in subsequent years, owing largely to the rail lines with which Carrollton became synonymous for years, a number of professionals also came to live in the area.

The city was officially incorporated in 1913 and, in subsequent years, became the hub of a succession of industries, including railway shipping, brick production and gravel distribution.

An amusing example of the city's quaint way of life and the pace at which it moved into the modern era is found in an article from 1928, wherein Carrollton proudly celebrated the completion of the installation of a modern sewer system. Carrollton Mayor F.M. Good was quoted as saying on this historic occasion, "We are in the midst of the greatest residential and industrial migration in the history of all time."[3]

Nine years later, in September of 1937, it was announced that the city's first traffic light would soon be installed.[4]

POPULATION BOOM

Owing to its economic opportunities, Carrollton's population exploded exponentially in the years following World War II. By 1950, the city's headcount was at 1,610. By 1960, it had more than doubled to 4,242, and by 1970 that number had tripled to 13,855. Within the next ten years, Carrollton's population increased by nearly 200%, and by 1980 it was at just under 41,000. That number would double again within the next two decades.

HOME TO MAJOR CORPORATIONS

Over the years, a number of major corporations have been headquartered in Carrollton, including BeautiControl Cosmetics, Halliburton Energy Services, International Paper, Mostek, and the Sarah Lee Bakery Group.

The reader should not presume, however, that Carrollton abandoned its agrarian roots with any sense of urgency. In fact, well into the 1980s, pasture land still existed within the city limits on which residents kept a nominal number of horses. As well, a fully functioning

3 "Carrollton folk celebrate start of sewer system," *The Dallas Morning News*, July 13, 1928.
4 "Carrollton to get traffic signal light," *The Carrollton Chronicle*, September 10, 1937.

Newman Smith High School in 2009
Beneath the tree is a marker placed in memory of Stacie and Susan
(Photo by Laura Marie Jimenez)

cattle ranch operated in the heart of one of the city's residential areas until just a few years ago. As Susan Smalley's friend, Deanna Bowman Sinclair, said of those days, "Nothing ever happened in Carrollton. It was a safe, cozy place to live."[5]

COMMITTED TO EDUCATION

Perhaps this safe and cozy atmosphere accounts for much of the city's perpetual population boom. Unquestionably, though, much of this growth in population post-1955 (the year in which the Carrollton and Farmers Branch school districts were merged) has been the result of the city's ongoing commitment to education. For a number of years, the Carrollton-Farmers Branch Independent School District was overseen by Superintendent Newman Smith, the namesake of the high school Stacie Madison and Susan Smalley attended.

FOR MANY YEARS, A SINGLE HIGH SCHOOL

Prior to the opening of Newman Smith High School, for a number of decades, the Carrollton-Farmers Branch Independent School District operated with but one secondary facility. That was Carrollton High School, which was originally the home of the Yellow Jackets. In 1934, however, the name was dropped in favor of the more menacing "Lions."[6]

In the early 1960s, the school district decided it was time for "Lion Country" to move to a new home. So, it was determined, a new high school would be built. Carrollton High School was converted into a junior high school. It still operates today under the name DeWitt Perry Middle School.

The new high school was opened in 1962 and christened "R.L. Turner High School" in honor of Robert Leon Turner, the school district's longtime superintendent who had passed away in June of that same year.[7]

NEWMAN SMITH HIGH SCHOOL

For a number of years, Turner High School served the City of Carrollton well. In the early 1970s, however, with the city's population swelling to nearly 14,000 and resident pushing further northward, it

---

5 Deanna Bowman Sinclair, October 1, 2009.
6 "The Lion's Tale slashes onto stage," *The Dallas Morning News*, October 5, 1934.
7 "Rites set for area schoolman," *The Dallas Morning News*, June 12, 1962.

Newman Smith High School in 2009
(Photo by Laura Marie Jimenez)

was decided the city could no longer function with just one high school.

In 1975, Newman Smith High School, the home of the Trojans, was launched in memory of another former school district superintendent. The first year it opened, the school was home to 8th and 9th Grade students only and subsequently added a grade each year. So it was, with its green and gold athletic uniforms standing in stark contrast to Turner's blue and white, Smith graduated its first senior class four years later in 1979.

A GOOD NATURED RIVALRY

In the first few years that Smith was opened, a good natured rivalry – sometimes referred to as "The Battle of Josey Lane" – raged between the two schools as Turner students worked hard to remind Smith's students that Turner was in Carrollton first.

This rivalry appears to have dissipated over the years, as other high schools have opened in the Carrollton area. But while it was alive and well, this rivalry occasionally resulted in schoolboy pranks, such as inthe early 1980s when students from Smith painted the bell on Turner's front lawn green and gold.

A RECORD OF ACADEMIC EXCELLENCE

What the high schools in the Carrollton/Farmers Branch area have in common is a record of academic excellence, especially Newman Smith High School. In its quarter century history, Newman Smith High School has accumulated some impressive statistics. Since 1975, the school has graduated National Merit Semifinalists, Rhodes Scholars, Academic Decathlon members, and winners of the Gates Millennium Scholar Award, AP Scholar Award and Dell Scholarship Award.

At last tally, less than 1% of the school's students drop out, and 97% of its student body receives their diplomas. As well, an impressive 92% of students go on to attend college.

In terms of SAT scores, the school's standards are well above the national average, as 88% of the students engage in Advanced Placement courses.

The school has been recognized repeatedly in *Texas Monthly* and *Newsweek* magazines as one of the best high schools not only in Texas but in the nation.

Smith is also one of the few high schools in America to offer Chinese language courses.[8]

---

8 Joe Pouncy, September 18, 2009 and
http://cfbstaff.cfbisd.edu/smith/smith_facts_f08.htm.

SHAWN SUTHERLAND

Newman Smith High School in 2009
(Photo by Laura Marie Jimenez)

These are but a few of the school's remarkable standards and statistics.

It is not surprising that Stacie Madison and Susan Smalley were right at home in such an impressive scholastic environment.

12

"I REALLY MISS THAT"

"I saw my friends coming out of band today, and I really miss that."

When 14 year old Stacie Madison and 15 year old Susan Smalley began attending Newman Smith High School in the fall of 1984, the student body totaled approximately 2,500 students.[1] The school had been in operation for nine years and had graduated five senior classes. One of these was the Class of 1982 to which I belonged.

The girls' worlds and mine, however, could not have been further removed.

YOUNGER THAN THAT NOW

Nearly three decades removed from them, I look back on my own high school days and shake my head in astonishment at the young man who was so needlessly intense and unnecessarily introspective.

During my time at the school, I was more at ease observing life than experiencing it and spent most of my time at Smith trying simply to disappear into the building's walls.

Having endured the death of a parent much younger than one should, I found my adolescent voice in the dark prose of Truman Capote's *In Cold Blood*, James Leo Herlihy's *Midnight Cowboy*, Jack Kerouac's *On the Road*, Eugene O'Neill's *Long Day's Journey into Night*, and Joseph Wambaugh's *The Onion Field*.

I studied rock and roll lyrics the way one would study the Bible and took flight – once upon a time – in the existentialism of The Doors, the mysticism of Richie Havens, The Moody Blues and Van Morrison, and the angst-fueled lyrics of Bruce Springsteen and Jim Steinman.

I feared anything that smacked of extra-curricular activity. There were no exceptions, not even when the journalism teacher told me that I had a gift with words and should be part of the high school's newspaper staff. I justified this asinine decision – one I have since

---

1 Joe Pouncy, September 18, 2009.

Portrait of the author as a young man
Senior year at Newman Smith High School in 1982

regretted – by reminding myself that, in a world where videotape recorders were not yet common, being part of any such after-school activity would interfere with such all important activities as watching afternoon reruns of Rod Serling's *The Twilight Zone*.

Thankfully, we live, we learn, and we grow. Perhaps Thomas Wolfe phrased it best when he said, "Man's youth is a wonderful thing. It is so full of anguish and of magic and he never comes to know it as it is, until it has gone from him forever."[2] Or as Bob Dylan once said, "I was so much older then; I'm younger than that now."[3]

TWO RESPECTFUL HIGH SCHOOL GIRLS

Stacie Madison and Susan Smalley, in contrast, started high school with an enthusiasm and passion for being involved in activities that never left them.

Stacie played the French horn in band and twirled the baton competitively while Susan played volleyball, basketball, and ran track. In the meantime, they both maintained higher than average grades.

Consequently, given their personable natures, It is not surprising that the girls' disappearances rocked the student body at Newman Smith High School.

C. Kenneth Dockray, Smith's Director of Orchestral Activities for many years, remembers the girls' disappearances and recalls, "Everyone was in complete shock over the incident."[4] As well, more than one person told me that they simply could not believe the situation was real.

Robert Hembree, currently the only teacher at Newman Smith High School to hold the distinction of having taught at the facility since the day it opened, remembers the atmosphere of the school as being, "very somber in the days right after their disappearances."[5]

In 1988, Joe Pouncy was a new economics and social studies teacher at Smith. Stacie and Susan both were in his classes at the time they disappeared. Today, he is the principal at the school. When I asked him about Stacie and Susan, Mr. Pouncy told me he remembers two girls who were well-liked and who improved the environment of the school's campus simply by being on it. What he recalled most, though, was the respect with which both girls treated their classmates and teachers. "It's something," admits Pouncy, "when kids respect you."[6]

---

2 Thomas Wolfe, *Of Time and the River*, Charles Scribner's Sons, 1935, p. 460.
3 Bob Dylan, "My Back Pages," Copyright Registration EP0000195713.
4 C. Kenneth Dockray, July 16, 2009.
5 Robert Hembree, August 12, 2009.
6 Joe Pouncy, September 18, 2009.

He also recalls that, when the girls disappeared, "It was like losing a family member."[7]

GRIEVING A LOSS

Many of the students at Smith joined Pouncy in feeling they had lost someone close to them when Stacie and Susan disappeared. They were, whether they realized it or not, grieving a loss.

Crystal Rainwater-Roberson told me, "I had known Stacie and Susan both for many years and was truly heartbroken when they went missing."[8]

It was as if an emotional earthquake had hit the school and, as is often the case following a disaster, people gathered together in what was the equivalent of a rescue effort.

BAND KIDS

During her junior year in high school, Stacie had reluctantly given up baton twirling at the insistence of her boyfriend, Jason Lawton, who wanted her to spend more time with him.[9] The next year, as a senior, she had joined the school's vocational education program and quickly learned she could not work the job she had taken at Dr. Jeffrey Adelglass' office, keep up with band, and maintain her grades. So, since money talks, band was eliminated. It was a decision Stacie would come to regret.

"*I saw my friends coming out of band today, and I really miss that.*" Those words come from Stacie Madison's diary, which Ida located in her daughter's room within days of her disappearance.[10]

Stacie's band mates apparently missed her too, and it was they who, more so than anyone else, worked tirelessly to spread the word about her disappearance. Recalls Jon Bohls, former Head Band Director at Newman Smith High School:

> The band kids took it upon themselves to do something. I think that they may have thought that there was not enough of an effort being made to find Stacie and Susan. Stacie was part of the family, and they wanted to have her back.[11]

---

7 Id.
8 Crystal Rainwater-Roberson, June 2, 2009.
9 *The Dallas Morning News*, August 19, 2001.
10 Ida Madison, June 20, 2009.
11 Jon Bohls, July 17, 2009.

The result was impressive. "Those kids came together," Ida Madison told me in June of 2009. "They plastered posters all over Carrollton and Farmers Branch about Stacie and Susan."

This gesture was not lost on Ida Madison or Carolyn Smalley.

THE MISSING POSTERS

"Both mothers said the Carrollton community has rallied to provide support for both families," reported *The Dallas Morning News* one week following the girls' disappearances. "Fliers bearing photographs of the teen-agers and a telephone number to call with information," said the paper, "have been distributed with pizza boxes and company newsletters." Fliers were also "placed inside of [a Kroger] store next to ads that are offered for shoppers."[12]

These fliers were also displayed prominently in the windows of many restaurants and stores in and around Carrollton and Farmers Branch.

One such establishment to display the girls' missing poster on its glass front door was everyone's favorite Mom and Pop record store, the Happening Sound Shop, which, in the years since its closing, has gained near mythological status in the memories of its former customers.

For those who lived in Carrollton during the 1970s through the 1990s, Happening Sound was in many ways both talisman and sentinel for the youth of the city. Consequently, since it serves as an encapsulated vision of the city's history during that era, the reader will have to abide a brief digression as the story of Happening Sound and Bill Allen are briefly recounted here, if only to offer the reader a momentary glimpse into how quaint the City of Carrollton was once upon a time.

BILL ALLEN AND HAPPENING SOUND

"Happening Sound, where nothing ever happens."

That was the catchphrase Bill Allen, the owner of Happening Sound Shop, would offer first time customers who asked him to whom they should make their check payable.

This was but one of at least half a dozen slogans Bill uttered daily during the 20-plus years he operated the beloved store that sold records, tapes, posters, guitars, record needles, guitar strings, sheet music, songbooks, woodwind reeds, and T-shirts.

Other aphorisms offered by the man who looked like *Star Trek*'s Dr. McCoy included the greetings "Hey, Gold Dust" for young men, while

---

12 *The Dallas Morning News*, March 30, 1988.

young women were invariably addressed as "Suga' Booga." These salutations were generally always followed by the words, "Do you need me to help you pick out about ten good ones today, or do you just want to look?" Bill's most famous tagline, though, was offered upon the completion of a sales transaction involving cash – "Change back - just like McDonald's."

"DADDY TRULY LOVED HIS CUSTOMERS"

To readers who did not know him, Bill's adages no doubt seem old fashioned and cornball. For his countless loyal customers, though, this was not important. What mattered was that they understood Bill had not incorporated his choice phrases into his repertoire by chance. Instead, they grasped that endearments such as "gold dust" reflected the reality that Bill was a person who saw the best in everyone and chose to envision everyone living up to their true potential. Consequently, those who comprehended this truth suspended cynicism because they knew Bill's sayings were just one part of the total experience of shopping at Happening Sound, as were his cigarettes, the store's punch cards that afforded shoppers a free album or single after the purchase of ten, and the knowledge that Bill would know you not only by your first name but by your musical tastes.

"Daddy truly loved his customers," Bill's daughter, Lisa Allen Foley, said when interviewed for this book. "I think that was the secret to his success...I can count on one hand the times I heard my father speak ill of anyone."[13]

A COMPLEX MAN

What most of Bill's customers, who remained with him as chain stores such as Peaches and Sound Warehouse came and went, never knew is that he was a much more complex and educated man than he ever let on.

Born to an impoverished Tennessee sharecropper in 1933, Floyd Allen grew up one of nine children. He came by the nickname "Bill" when he raised a billy goat as part of a Future Farmers of America project in high school. Farming was not in Bill's future, though, and following a stint on a U.S. Navy aircraft carrier during the Korean war, he worked days and studied engineering in the evenings at Lamar University. Eventually receiving his degree in that field, Bill worked for a number of years as the manager of an industrial production facility. This career he continued for some time, even after he and his wife Marie (whom he referred to as "the brains of the operation") opened

---

13 Lisa Allen Foley, July 22, 2009.

their first record store in 1972. "My mom was every bit as wonderful as my Dad," Lisa Allen Foley told me, "and frankly, I don't think he ever really recovered from her death at age 50 in 1983."[14]

NOTHING LASTS FOREVER

Sadly, nothing lasts forever.

Happening Sound remained in business until 1994 and only closed its doors when Bill Allen, after a lifetime of heavy smoking, was diagnosed with a cancer that took him quickly.

I do not recall any fanfare accompanying the passing of Bill Allen and Happening Sound. Yet I would argue that Bill touched as many lives as any retailer whose obituaries made the newspaper's front page.

Today, 15 years after his death, faces still ignite with smiles as people discuss their memories of shopping with Bill and – as if he were a character from *The Andy Griffith Show* come to life – the comfort they took in knowing he would always greet them with the same words he employed for more than 20 years.

With Bill's passing, an era in Carrollton ended. In any number of ways, he represented the city's innocence, its rural roots, and a slower time when a storekeeper actually took the time required to get to know his patrons.

In 2009, Bill Allen and what he represents are sorely missed, and I do not anticipate a day will ever come when I do not regret that I can no longer pile into my car, drive to Happening Sound, and be greeted with a friendly and familiar, "Well, hello, Gold Dust!"

---

14 Id.

Carrollton legend Bill Allen
(Photo courtesy of Bryan Pruner)

13

ONCE UPON A TIME
ON FOREST LANE

Lost boys and golden girls
Down on the corner and all around the world
It doesn't matter where they're going or wherever they've been
'Cause they got one thing in common, it's true
They'll never let a night like tonight go to waste...[1]

The missing posters were also plastered on the glass doors and drive-thru windows of the fast food restaurants located on a two mile stretch of North Dallas roadway that, at the time of the girls' disappearances in 1988, had already been synonymous with teenage fun for more than two decades – Forest Lane.

A LITERAL CROSS SECTION OF DALLAS LIFE

Forest Lane begins in Garland, Texas at the intersection of Avenue D and South Garland Avenue. If one is traveling east to west, it runs for a little more than 14 miles before it ends, in the shadow of Interstate Highway 35, at Harry Hines Boulevard. At this point, Forest Lane becomes Reeder Road, which is home to countless warehouses and industrial businesses.

When traveling the 14 miles that comprise Forest Lane, one will behold a literal cross section of Dallas life, including everything from the homes of the very rich to those of the not so rich, as well as hospitals, warehouses, strip shopping centers and restaurants.

Seven miles west of its starting point in Garland, Texas, Forest Lane intersects with Central Expressway, the site of the once legendary Gemini Drive-In. The Gemini, although once as much a part of the teen landscape as Forest Lane, has since been bulldozed and replaced by a succession of uninspiring fast food restaurants.

Four miles further west, one can view, between Midway and Rosser Roads, the infamous mural created by the W.T. White High School graduating Class of 1976 in an effort to cover over a litany of

---

1 Jim Steinman, "Lost Boys and Golden Girls," Copyright Registration V3519 D594 P1-2.

obscene graffiti. The images depicted on the wall include everything from spaceships to pinballs and pointed forefingers discharging electricity. The common theme running through all of these elements - which seem like some homage to the film *Tommy* - is that they are all expressions of the mid-1970s teenage vision of a future wherein toe socks, skateboarding, T-shirts, Pet Rocks, mood rings, 8 track tapes, black light posters, and winged haircuts were celebrated as embodiments of a brighter future.

When painting it in the relative innocence of 1976, the wall's creators no doubt never envisioned that one day the street that served as an icon of carefree fun for their generation would become forever linked with the disappearances of Stacie Madison and Susan Smalley.

At the time the mural was painted, Forest Lane, and particularly the two mile subsection of the street between Midway Road and Webbs Chapel Road, which served as its beating heart, was the embodiment of the sheer joy of youth.

A DIFFERENT TIME IN AMERICA

This was, quite simply, a different time in America, as Newman Smith High School's policy about smoking on campus in the 1970s and 1980s demonstrated.

Namely, as insane as it sounds in the politically correct world of the 21st century, the school actually had a fenced-in center courtyard which served as its "smoking area." Presumably, the logic behind this policy was that having such a designated area would minimize damage done to school property by students who would otherwise be smoking in areas such as bathrooms.

In order to police underage smoking, the school issued smoking passes at the beginning of the semester to those students who were old enough in the eyes of the State of Texas to buy cigarettes. The wallet size card distributed to students served as a license to smoke cigarettes between classes free from hassle.

For faculty, this was often a cross to bear. As if they were not already over tasked, certain teachers were assigned the unenviable chore of patrolling the smoking area for underage smokers.

It was in this world, where adults turned a blind eye to teenage smoking, that Forest Lane was cruised.

CRUISING FOREST

I have heard it said that writers should write about what they know. If this is the case, I must admit that, since I was too busy working while in high school, when not living under a rock, I never once "cruised"

The former Park Forest Movie Theater on Forest Lane,
known today as the North Dallas Antique Mall
(Photo by Laura Marie Jimenez)

Forest Lane. However, during the research phase of this book, I was thankfully able to find people willing to indulge my quest to comprehend the magic and allure the street once held.

Samantha Judge (Newman Smith Class of 1983) remembers her nights with friends on Forest Lane fondly. She explained that:

> Forest Lane was the local hangout for kids in high school. Everyone cruised up and down Forest Lane at all hours of the night. Usually, people would head out there on Fridays and Saturdays around 7:00 p.m. and hang out until midnight to 2:00 a.m. There were lots of food establishments up and down the road. Everyone would find "their" particular group of friends, then park there for the evening and hang out.[2]

Jill J. Farrer (W.T. White Class of 1978) said of Forest Lane:

> The closest example I can think of is the movie *American Graffiti*, but for me it was 1976-1980. Stop lights, cruising at five miles per hour (slow enough to have conversations with the cars moving next to you), Chinese fire drills, changing cars, pulling over to hang out, people walking up and down Forest Lane…going through drive-thrus for fast food backwards in your car.[3]

A Chinese fire drill, by the way, is an exercise in pure folly (generally conducted by teenage girls) where the occupants of a given car will exit the vehicle at a red light, run around it in a circle, and then pile back inside of it before the light turns green.

Speaking of cars, the extent to which they were an integral part of the Forest Lane scene cannot be overstated.

STREET RACING

Lonnie Lutz (J.J. Pearce Class of 1973) says Forest Lane has been popular with teenagers since at least the 1960s because, in addition to the numerous fast food establishments on the strip, the stop lights were approximately one quarter mile apart – ideal for street racing.[4]

Of the street racing, Edward L. Williams (R.T. Turner Class of 1977) adds:

2 Samantha Judge, June 13, 2009.
3 Jill J. Farrer, June 9, 2009.
4 Lonnie Lutz, October 13, 2009.

In the 1973/1974 time frame, people brought out real "Funny Cars" on trailers and would drag race those monsters. One issue of *Hot Rod* magazine (or one of the street car magazines) even featured Forest Lane and the crazy racing that went on.[5]

In this regard, said one man, "If Forest Lane was dead, you would go to Emerald Street or California Crossing, where people would line the streets and watch drag races." Concerning these two streets that have become as iconic as Forest Lane, when I interviewed him, Sergeant John W. Crawford of the Carrollton Police Department also spoke of the illegal street races on Emerald Street:

> The drag racers would go to Emerald Street down in Dallas. There's a stretch of Emerald Street that's Dallas, then it goes to Farmers Branch, and then they would come up Luna Road to Carrollton. Dallas would run them off. Farmers Branch would run them off. They'd come up here to Carrollton, and we'd run them back down to Dallas. It was this big circle with the racers. So, tied in with Forest Lane was the Emerald Racers. People would come from all over the Metroplex to race cars.[6]

Edward L. Williams remembers the Emerald races well, but also recalls an earlier time when street racing actually occurred on Forest Lane proper. This, however, was a thing of the past by 1976, according to Mr. Williams, who said:

> The high profile racing on Forest Lane was shut down after several street racers lost their lives on the strip. By 1977, it was just normal kids doing a little low profile street racing...the more serious racing moved down to Emerald – where several people were killed over the next few years.[7]

Samantha Judge also recalls the dark side of Emerald Street:

> I was present one night when a kid on a motorcycle decided to race a car. He was killed...the sad part about that night was that everyone was so scared of getting in trouble that everyone left the scene. Only a handful of people stuck

5 Edward L. Williams, July 17, 2009.
6 John W. Crawford, June 4, 2009.
7 Edward L. Williams, July 31, 2009.

The Arby's restaurant on Forest Lane
(Photo by Laura Marie Jimenez with the kind
permission of the Arby's Restaurant Group, Inc.)

around until the ambulance and police showed up. It was the saddest thing I had ever witnessed. That is when I quit going to Emerald Street.[8]

When I spoke with David Abbey (W.T. White Class of 1984) about the racing scene on Forest Lane in the early 1980s, he told me:

When I started going out there, it was still pretty innocent. Everyone was there just to have a good time. I was there just to have a good time. For me, it was about the cars and street racing. So, that was the group I was involved with.

Abbey continued by saying that in the early 1980s:

The feel of Forest Lane was changing...there seemed to be more and more people showing up every weekend. With the increased numbers, the police, who had previously just watched, began to try to control the scene.

One of the ways in which the police began to take control was an increased police presence and signs prohibiting parking. "The group that I was hanging out with," said Abbey, "moved our activities away from Forest Lane and down to Emerald Street."

The racing scene on Emerald Street, laments Abbey, was soon discovered by non-racers who were "more into loud stereos and drinking" than anything else.[9] The result, says Abbey, was that the racing scene moved even farther away from Forest Lane – to Manana Road and California Crossings.

HAVING A BLAST

Not everything on Forest Lane was about racing, though. In fact, there were often times when there was so much traffic on Forest Lane that racing would have been next to impossible. As Susan Lott Wheeler (W.T. White Class of 1973) remembered:

I was one of the hundreds who would cruise Forest Lane Friday and Saturday nights in the early 1970s. The strip would run from about halfway between Marsh Lane and Webbs Chapel Road all the way east to Inwood Road, and the traffic would be nearly bumper to bumper.[10]

8 Samantha Judge, August 2, 2009.
9 David Abbey, August 3, 2009.
10 Susan Lott Wheeler, February 8, 2009.

The former Park Forest Movie Theater on Forest Lane,
known today as the North Dallas Antique Mall
(Photo by the author)

"There were always so many kids cruising Forest Lane that sometimes you had a hard time locating your friends," said Samantha Judge, "but you definitely made new ones along the way."[11]

If this sounds like fun, according to those who lived it, that word does not even begin to describe the carefree socializing that transpired on the street in those days.

"Forest Lane was what we did for entertainment," said Paula Thomas Allen (R.L. Turner Class of 1975). "We hung out, raced, and met new people. I went there anytime I was able."[12]

Kelli Hargrove Barton (R.L. Turner Class of 1986) concurs with this statement and says, "No matter what I was doing on the weekend, I always ended up on Forest Lane. I met some of the greatest people cruising Forest."[13]

"It was easy," said Edward L. Williams "to meet people, and the kids kind of hung out in different cliques."[14]

Cathy Carrell Parker (W.T. White Class of 1973) recalled, "Every Friday night we were out there meeting people and having a blast!"[15]

And what a blast it reportedly was. Lori Pepsis Baker (W.T. White Class of 1978) remembers her days on Forest Lane with obvious fondness, and listed some of the memories that came quickly to mind:

> The Chinese Fire Drills...a best friend who streaked down Forest Lane...there was a "head shop" and we all thought it was cooly dangerous just to go look at the blacklight posters.[16]

Edward L. Williams remembers:

> There was a big shopping store – FedMart, I think – where most of the kids hung out, and live bands would come and set up and play all night for free. It was some party! By the time I started driving in 1976, the police had started cracking down, and the FedMart was plastered with "No Loitering" signs. The bands were gone.[17]

Williams recalls there was still plenty of socializing after the demise of the free concerts, though, and says:

---

11 Samantha Judge, August 2, 2009.
12 Paula Thomas Allen, July 12, 2009.
13 Kelli Hargrove Barton, April 16, 2009.
14 Edward L. Williams, July 27, 2009.
15 Cathy Carrell Parker, April 10, 2009.
16 Lori Baker, June 8, 2009.
17 Edward L. Williams, July 17, 2009.

The Mustang Club, which I hung with, camped out in the Burger King parking lot right off Marsh Lane and Forest Lane and was just out there to look at and show off the cars…and maybe get lucky and meet some girls along the way.[18]

Mark Blythe (Newman Smith Class of 1980) recalls equally mellow evenings, such as those spent hanging "out in the Hannah's Pies parking lot all night listening to 'My Sharona.'"[19]

CERTAIN GROUPS OF KIDS WOULD DRINK OR DO DRUGS

Granted, pies were not the only thing consumed on Forest Lane.

Stacy Robinson (Newman Smith Class of 1984) said, "Who could forget the classic statement, 'Where's the party?'"[20]

In the same manner, insofar as Forest Lane went, Samantha Judge admits, "Sometimes certain groups of kids would drink or do drugs."[21]

One individual who wished to remain anonymous, and whom I will refer to as "Scott," spoke of how everyone who cruised Forest Lane thought they were cool, especially an enterprising young man named Robbie Van Winkle who would:

> …pull up behind the Handy Dan hardware store in his truck with a keg in the back and sell beer for $1.00 a cup. You would have upwards of 100 to 150 people in the parking lot. Then the cops would show up, and people would scatter and go back to cruising.[22]

Robbie Van Winkle would, of course, within just a few short years, rechristen himself "Vanilla Ice" before scoring a nationwide hit by repackaging Queen's "Under Pressure" as "Ice Ice Baby."

YOU THOUGHT EVERYONE WAS YOUR FRIEND

For the most part, though, as Captain Greg Ward of the Frisco Police Department told me, the Forest Lane scene was primarily about high school kids just blowing off steam and socializing.[23]

Consequently, even though there was the occasional report of drunkards threatening others with violence, people simply trusted each

---

18 Id.
19 Mark Blythe, March 31, 2009.
20 Stacy Robinson, February 26, 2009.
21 Samantha Judge, June 9, 2009.
22 "Scott," July 17, 2009.
23 Greg Ward, June 16, 2009.

The Arby's restaurant on Forest Lane
(Photo by Laura Marie Jimenez with the kind
permission of the Arby's Restaurant Group, Inc.)

in those days in a manner that is foreign to the America of 2009. Lori Pepsi Baker (W.T. White Class of 1978) says:

> The thing with Forest Lane was that, as a kid, you thought everyone was your friend and everyone was there for the same reason. Even if you weren't all from the same school, you just figured they were just like you - only from somewhere else.[24]

The result was that people on Forest Lane were not afraid to allow strangers into their cars and had no fear of accepting rides from people they did not know. In fact, stated Scott, people even thought nothing of venturing to house parties at the invitation of people whom they did not know and who they were likely to never see again.

Towards the middle 1980s, however, says David Abbey:

> *Carcraft* magazine ran an article naming Forest Lane as one of the Top Ten Cruise Spots in the nation. I recall there were people showing up from Oklahoma and points further away to cruise Forest Lane after the article came out.

After that, Abbey told me, Forest Lane "went from being very *American Graffiti*-like to something very different, almost cold and unfriendly."[25]

NEVER THE SAME

Most youths on Forest Lane, unfortunately, were oblivious to this change.

That was before March 20, 1988 and the disappearances of Stacie Madison and Susan Smalley, both of whom – at least according to *The Dallas Morning News* – "often went to the Forest Lane area...to meet other young people."[26]

For many, the event marked a turning point in the history of Forest Lane.

Carol Lynn Cowan Bockes acknowledges that the night on which Stacie Madison and Susan Smalley disappeared was:

> The only incident of that nature...but after that occured, Forest

---

24 Lori Baker, June 9, 2009.
25 David Abbey, August 3, 2009.
26 *The Dallas Morning News*, March 24, 1988.

Lane was never the same. Once upon a time, we could meet anyone, give them a ride without fear...we will never have that again...oh, gosh, to have those days again.[27]

Kelli Hargrove Barton agrees, adding, "When I and my friends used to cruise Forest Lane, we felt very safe, but bad things can happen in the best of neighborhoods."[28]

In hindsight, Lori Pepsis Baker looks back on those days with gratitude, as she acknowledges that the dynamics of Forest Lane were a "perfect set-up for any kind of predator, and we didn't even use that word back then."[29] Kelly Driskell Wells (R.L. Turner Class of 1986), who declared "I would kill my daughters if they just jumped in the car with strangers like we did!," obviously shares Lori Pepsi Baker's opinion.[30]

Michelle Bolig Huber says:

Some had thought Stacie and Susan got into a car with the wrong people on Forest Lane. I just can't see them jumping into a car with some shady characters. If they did get in a car with guys, they must have appeared normal, which scares me even more. How dumb were we back then, jumping in and out of strangers' cars on Forest Lane?[31]

ONCE UPON A TIME IN AMERICA

That was truly once upon a time in America when life was different from the way it is today. "We had no fear back then," remembers Stefanie Brown (R.L. Turner Class of 1987), who observed, "I'm surprised more of us didn't end up hurt back then. Maybe the psychos were in hiding and we all just got lucky. It was an age of innocence."[32]

Today, says Captain Greg Ward, online communities such as Facebook have replaced the cruising practices of old, so the glory days of Forest Lane exist only in the memories of those who lived them.[33] "The mural, the Burger King, and a few other landmarks stand out like historical monuments to those who remember the times," says Edward L. Williams. "To everyone else, they are just burger joints and fences."[34]

---

27 Carol Lynn Cowan Bockes, June 8, 2009.
28 Kelli Hargrove Barton, June 9, 2009.
29 Lori Baker, January 7, 2009.
30 Kelly Driskell Wells, March 16, 2009.
31 Michelle Bolig Huber, February 23, 2009.
32 Stefanie Brown, January 23, 2009.
33 Greg Ward, June 16, 2009.
34 Edward L. Williams, July 31, 2009.

The Arby's restaurant on Forest Lane
(Photo by Laura Marie Jimenez with the kind
permission of the Arby's Restaurant Group, Inc.)

14

BAD DREAMS

I can only imagine what dreams
Carolyn Smalley and Ida Madison have endured.

I have a confession to make. I had a nightmare the other night.

It is obviously an outpouring of spending too many hours contemplating missing girls.

In the dream, I am on the outskirts of the parking lot of the strip center at Forest Lane and Webbs Chapel Road where Stacie Madison's car was recovered.

It is somewhere deep in the night. The city is asleep, but I am here to peer into the past.

The wind howls like some forlorn spirit. The clouds in the night sky drift above and reflect the light of the moon, which disappears behind the clouds and then reappears.

These sights and sounds do not frighten me. I have been in this parking lot many times in my lifetime.

Suddenly, I sense that a beast is following me. No matter how quickly I walk, I cannot evade this phantom. I turn to see what is behind me, but nothing is there.

Now I am very afraid.

My breathing increases and I can hear my heart beating.

Then, I realize why I am so upset. I know what night this is, where I am, and what has been following me.

I am standing inside of March 20, 1988, the night on which Stacie Madison and Susan Smalley disappeared.

I am but a few feet away from the girls' last moments of liberty.

Then the entity is somehow ahead of me. Still, I cannot see it. I know it is drawing ever nearer to Stacie's car.

The girls are exiting Stacie's Mustang. They are speaking softly to one another about their plans. Were the wind not so loud, perhaps I could hear the words uttered in the distance, but I cannot.

The wind is not the only problem. I try to walk, but it is as if my feet are in molasses.

I now see a second car in the parking lot. I am determined to reach the girls before they climb into this other car that embodies their destiny.

Finally, I am upon Stacie and Susan, but it is too late. They are already in this monster's car.

There is still another person outside of this second car, but they are outside of my field of vision. I know it is the entity, now in human form, responsible for so much anguish.

Suddenly, my subconscious reminds me that, although I am temporarily within 1988, my life is in 2009. I know I am inside of a dream and realize my mind is trying to awaken me.

Who is this person that I cannot see, that I do not wish to see but must? I am determined to know, and I turn on my heels to seize a glimpse of this creature.

I reach out my hand to touch the back of the entity's shoulder. I brace myself in anticipation of what I will see when it turns to acknowledge me. I know I am about to see the face of evil.

I awaken with a start.

It is hours before the sun will rise, but I know I will not sleep again this night.

I can only imagine what dreams Carolyn Smalley and Ida Madison have endured since 1988.

15

RECONSTRUCTING THE NIGHT

The department's next best alternative was to create a detailed inventory of Stacie Madison's and Susan Smalley's activities.

Regrettably, the missing posters, television news reports, and newspaper articles combined generated nothing in the way of information that police could use.

Instead, those efforts seemed only to spark calls from citizens that led police down blind alleys and towards dead ends.

Reflecting on the reaction the high profile nature of the case provoked, Captain Greg Ward recalls, "A lot of it was sightings. We got a lot of people wanting to help, people wanting to help search. A few weirdoes came out of the bushes, but they all meant well."[1]

Among these oddballs were individuals who phoned police for no reason other than to promote their own pet theories regarding what had happened to the girls. Even Ida Madison and Carolyn Smalley were not immune from these types and endured their own share of calls from eccentrics offering everything from well wishes to conjecture. Ida Madison actually kept a log of what she termed "strange telephone numbers."[2]

A CALL FROM A PERSON WHO KNEW THE TRUTH?

One such strange call came from an anonymous individual who refused to identify himself. His message, though, was eerily sinister, and he had bragged that he could offer specific information regarding what had become of the girls. Yet his approach was so unsettling that it filled the mother who received the call with an immediate desire to hang up the telephone. Through the telephone, the man had shouted, "Look lady – if you don't want to know what happened to your daughter," as the distraught woman informed him that she was ending the call. The man never called again and was, by default, classified as a prankster.

Another presumed joker called police on an unrecorded line five

---

1 Greg Ward, June 16, 2009.
2 Ida Madison, August 3, 2009.

days after the girls vanished and said, "Stacie and Susan are alright."[3]

Carolyn and Ida and the police lost count of the number of calls such as these that came in. Yet for all the times the telephone rang, the two people from whom everyone was hoping to hear (Stacie and Susan) never called.

What had become of them?

THREE THINGS SOLVE CRIMES

"[T]hree things solve crimes," says David Simon, author of the book *Homicide: A Year on the Killing Streets*, "Physical evidence. Witnesses. Confessions." Of this "detective's Holy Trinity," as Simon terms it, "Without one of the first two elements, there is little chance that detectives will find a suspect capable of providing the third."[4]

Meanwhile, Carrollton police faced the near impossible task of unraveling the mystery of the girls' disappearances with no confessions, no physical evidence beyond Stacie's Ford Mustang – which they had failed to fingerprint – and no known witnesses to the girls' activities or whereabouts beyond their a.m. sighting in the parking lot at the Steak and Ale on Belt Line Road and Sakowitz Drive in the wee hours of Sunday morning, March 20, 1988.

MY OWN RECONSTRUCTION

Given the hand dealt them, the department's next best alternative was to create a detailed inventory of Stacie Madison's and Susan Smalley's activities on the evening of Saturday, March 19, 1988 and the morning of Sunday, March 20, 1988. The hope was that, by cataloging the girls' movements, the police just might get lucky and uncover that one witness with whom the girls had discussed their plans for later that morning, who they were meeting, where they were going or what they might be doing.

The Carrollton Police Department's file on the Madison/Smalley case is rightfully off limits to me, as it is to all non-peace officers. Thus, the re-creation of the events of this pivotal night included here is created from the following sources: newspaper accounts gleaned from *The Dallas Morning News*, *The Dallas Times Herald* and *The Fort Worth Star-Telegram*; the limited information Captain Greg Ward and officers from the Carrollton Police Department were able to share with me; my interview with Carolyn Smalley; and my interview with Ida Madison during which the investigation conducted by the Madison family's private detective was discussed to limited degree.

---

3 *The Fort Worth Star-Telegram*, March 18, 1998.
4 David Simon, *Homicide: A Year on the Killing Streets*, Houghton Mifflin, 1991, p. 73.

This, then, is my own reconstruction of Stacie Madison's and Susan Smalley's last known activities.

AT THE MADISON HOUSEHOLD

The reader will recall that Saturday, March 19, 1988, came very early for Stacie Madison, who had taken the SAT exam that morning in anticipation of her upcoming freshman year at what was then North Texas State University.

Ida Madison cannot recall where the test was administered or the time at which it began. It was apparently offered at a locale in or close to Carrollton, though, for Carolyn Smalley, who worked that day at her part-time job at the Dillard's in Prestonwood Shopping Center, remembers Stacie and Susan together came to have lunch with her.

Afterwards, Stacie went home, where her mother gave her a home perm.

Then Susan had called to see what Stacie had planned for the evening.

ALMOST A TRIO

According to Deanna Bowman Sinclair, there had almost been three girls on the town that night.

"Susan was a best friend to me," Sinclair told me.

She and Susan had talked about getting together that Saturday night, but their plans had never gotten beyond the discussion stage.

"I was supposed to hang out with Stacie and Susan that night, but my parents would not let me go," said Sinclair. "It was my Dad's birthday, and I was so mad I could not go."[5]

If Stacie knew Sinclair had originally been a part of the plans for that night, she apparently did not deem it significant enough to mention it to Ida Madison, who had never heard of Mrs. Sinclair until September 2009.[6]

When queried by me regarding what Stacie and Susan had planned for that evening, Sinclair told me, "I don't remember that night being any different than any other...We never really set plans any night. We just went."[7]

---

5 Deanna Bowman Sinclair, September 28, 2009.
6 Ida Madison, September 28, 2009.
7 Deanna Bowman Sinclair, October 2, 2009.

Photo by Laura Marie Jimenez

YOU NEVER KNOW WHEN I'LL CALL

After her telephone conversation with Susan, Stacie washed the perm solution from her hair and dressed in her favorite white sweatshirt and white slacks.

Susan arrived at the Madisons' home to pick Stacie up around 5:00 p.m., and the two were soon heading towards the front door. Ida called for the girls to stop where they were and reminded Stacie that her midnight curfew was still in place, even if she was spending the night away from home.

"How will you know," joked one of the girls, "if we're there?" Ida's response was, "Because you never know when I'll call."[8]

While reviewing a draft of some of the chapters of this book, Ida told me, "When I read about Stacie, sometimes scenes flash through my head of things that happened with her." One such mental image was of:

> ...the time I stood on the front sidewalk and watched Stacie drive off by herself for the first time. I said a little prayer asking God to look after her...a similar scene played out [on March 19, 1988]...I watched her go, and never, ever thought that could be the last time I saw her.[9]

AT THE SMALLEYS' CONDOMINIUM – THE FIRST TIME

From the Madisons' home the girls caravanned to the Smalleys' condominium, which was located just a few miles to the east.

Susan, who was working two jobs and saving money to buy a new car, had taken Carolyn Smalley to work that morning and then spent much of the day running errands in her mother's car. Susan's mother's shift would soon be ending, and that meant it was time for her to travel to Prestonwood Shopping Center and pick up her mother. So, the girls parked Stacie's car near the Smalleys' home and drove to Prestonwood Shopping Center in Carolyn Smalley's car.

AT PRESTONWOOD MALL

"Susan took me to work that morning in my car," Carolyn Smalley told me, "and Stacie and Susan came and picked me up in my car, and [we] went back to my house."[10]

While at the mall, Stacie spent most of what money she had on the

---

8 *The Fort Worth Star-Telegram*, March 18, 1998.
9 Ida Madison, September 8, 2009.
10 Carolyn Smalley, July 14, 2009.

Photo by Laura Marie Jimenez

purchase of a pair of shoes at the Lord & Taylor Department Store. Along with Stacie's hot rollers, these shoes – still in the shopping bag - were discovered atop Susan Smalley's bed a day or so after the girls disappeared.[11]

The purchase of these shoes is significant and is mentioned here because this act stands as evidence that Stacie and Susan had no plans to run away on the night they disappeared. Instead, it proves they were just two young girls intent on enjoying a random Saturday night.

AT THE SMALLEY'S CONDOMINIUM – THE SECOND TIME

Carolyn Smalley too had plans for the evening. She had a date for which she needed to get ready. So, upon arriving at the Smalley household, the three ladies set about getting dressed up for a night out.

Soon enough, Stacie and Susan were dressed and ready for their evening of fun.

"I told them to be careful," Carolyn Smalley would recall, reflecting on her final moments with Stacie and Susan, "not knowing I'd never see them again"[12]

Carolyn Smalley told me, "I always look at March 19th as the day Susan disappeared, as this was the last day I saw her...if only you knew how often I wish I could go back to that night and change something, but I know I can't."[13] One of the things Carolyn says she wishes she could change involves her conviction that, "Everyone should always leave their loved ones with happy or kind words, as you never know when it will be the last time you ever see them."[14]

WHEREABOUTS UNKNOWN – THE FIRST TIME

From this point forward, tracking the girls' movements is at times simply impossible.

At only three points during this enigmatic window in time can the girls' whereabouts be established with any certainty (i.e., at approximately 10:00 p.m., midnight and sometime around 1:00 a.m.). The details of the rest of the evening are a mystery written in invisible ink.

Consequently, where Susan and Stacie were during the early part of the evening and why they were there will most likely never be

---

11 Ida Madison, June 20, 2009 and August 3, 2009.
12 *The Dallas Morning News*, August 19, 2001.
13 Carolyn Smalley, September 22, 2009.
14 Id.

known.

One certainty, however, is that by approximately 10:00 p.m. the girls were visiting with friends in an Arlington apartment. This we know thanks in part to the persistence of Ida Madison.

A MYSTERIOUS TELEPHONE CALL TO ARLINGTON

In the days following her daughter's disappearance, says Ida Madison, "I requested that the Smalley phone be checked for long distance calls."[15]   This request was prompted by a telephone conversation Ida had with a friend of Stacie's who lived in Arlington.

"I can't remember who introduced them," says Ida of this unidentified young man. "I'm thinking we all went to Six Flags and he met us there through prearrangement with a friend we knew."[16]

In 1998, *The Fort Worth Star-Telegram* described the individual in question as someone Stacie "may have been dating, a guy who told police he was trying to avoid Stacie before his girlfriend caught on."[17] But as far as Ida can recall, this boy was but one of several with whom "Stacie maintained telephone friendships."[18]

Regardless, Ida was convinced Stacie had telephoned the youth on the night of Saturday, March 19, 1988 and may have even traveled to his apartment.

"I called the boy who lived in Arlington," says Ida, "and he denied to me that Stacie had been there, but did tell me she called. He said he didn't know what time that was."[19]

Suspicious now that this young man was not being honest with her, Ida requested that the Smalleys' telephone records be checked. The inquiry revealed that someone inside the Smalleys' residence, presumably Stacie Madison, had placed a call to the boy's apartment at 12:01 a.m.[20]

A MYSTERIOUS TRIP TO ARLINGTON

Officers from the Carrollton Police Department, as well as a private investigator hired by the Madison family, interviewed the young man. Eventually, he admitted that Stacie and Susan had indeed visited his apartment that Saturday night for "a very short visit."[21] He would also acknowledge, Ida told me, "He lied to me because he didn't want to

15 Ida Madison, June 30, 2009.
16 Id.
17 *The Fort Worth Star-Telegram*, March 19, 1988.
18 Ida Madison, June 10, 2009.
19 Id., June 18, 2009.
20 The *Fort Worth Star-Telegram*, March 18, 1998.
21 Ida Madison, June 10, 2009.

get Stacie in trouble, and he knew I wouldn't have approved of her going over there."[22]

The hour at which Stacie and Susan traveled to Arlington in Stacie's Ford Mustang cannot be established. *The Fort Worth Star-Telegram* offers only that, "At some point during the evening, [Stacie and Susan] drove to Arlington and found an apartment full of people hanging out."[23] According to Ida Madison, though, "As I recall, there were four boys who lived in the apartment, and they were the only ones there to my knowledge. The girls went over, but declined to stay long."[24]

DRUGS OR ALCOHOL A FACTOR?

Perhaps the reason the Arlington visit ended early was because the girls discovered an unwelcome truth: according to gossip, the young man they visited was rumored to frequently smoke marijuana and possibly supplement his income by selling it to friends and acquaintances.

In 1998, Captain Greg Ward told the *The Fort Worth Star-Telegram* that Stacie and Susan both "were just normal teen-age girls. They liked to go out on Friday, Saturday nights, drink a little, smoke, you know?"[25] But this is contested by some.

Ultimately, the possibility of two teenage girls engaging in behavior that is typical of nearly all teenagers is irrelevant when compared to the reality that Stacie and Susan have been missing for nearly 22 years. When it comes to the subject of drugs and alcohol, though, Ida Madison contends:

> Stacie got drunk at a party one time. She came home, and I knew immediately that she had been drinking. She got so sick that she spent the night in the bathroom. She never drank again. One of her friends told me that at parties where liquor was offered, Stacie would take a drink and then pour it in the nearest potted plant. The police told me that when they were in Arlington at the boys' apartment that night, the boys were drinking beer and offered the girls some pot. The boys told them Stacie did not accept either...I repeatedly told the police that if they heard something along those lines about my daughter, I wanted to know. I did not want to read something in the paper, as I did more than once, that I didn't already

22 Id., June 18, 2009.
23 *The Fort Worth Star-Telegram*, March 18, 1998.
24 Ida Madison, June 18, 2009.
25 *The Fort Worth Star-Telegram*, March 18, 1998.

know. They assured me they were telling me all they knew. I just had to resolve myself to that fact that, if I wanted publicity about the case, I had to deal with the untruths that popped up. We had a hard time with that, but for us that was a necessary evil when it came to finding the one person who had a real answer for us.[26]

In this regard, Michelle Bolig Huber offers, "I recall seeing Stacie and Susan at several parties in high school. They never got wild or crazy, so I was very shocked to hear about their disappearances."[27]

LEAVING ARLINGTON

Returning to the events of the night of Saturday, March 19, 1988, Stacie and Susan left the boy's apartment in short order, saying that they intended to go eat a late dinner at a Chili's restaurant. They also intimated that they might return to the apartment at a later hour.[28]

JASON LAWTON WALKS HOME

Meanwhile, in Carrollton, Jason Lawton's evening shift at McDonald's ended at 10:45 p.m.[29]

Stacie, Lawton says, had taken him to work earlier that day. His car, depending upon which story one hears, was either in the shop with a broken fly wheel or had been repossessed. Either way, Lawton presumed Stacie would be coming that night to give him a ride home after work. She never materialized.[30]

A confused Lawton called the Madison household – presumably from McDonald's – and asked if Stacie was there. "Jason thought Stacie was coming to pick him up," recalls Ida Madison. "I told him she was out for the evening when he called me, as [Stacie] asked me to do."[31] Nevertheless, Lawton claims, he waited at McDonald's for at least an hour in the hopes that Stacie might appear before walking home and going to bed.[32]

AT THE SMALLEY'S CONDOMINIUM – THE THIRD TIME

Around the time that Jason Lawton was allegedly walking home,

26 Ida Madison, June 9, 2009.
27 Michelle Bolig Huber, August 10, 2009.
28 *The Fort Worth Star-Telegram*, March 18, 1998.
29 Id.
30 Jason Lawton, July 15, 2009.
31 Ida Madison, June 18, 2009.
32 Jason Lawton, July 15, 2009 and *The Fort Worth Star-Telegram*, March 18, 1998.

A 2009 photo of the now defunct Addison, Texas
Steak and Ale on Belt Line Road and Sakowitz Drive
(Photo by the author)

Stacie and Susan were returning to the Smalley condominium after their trek to Arlington. This we know because at 12:01 a.m., a person within the Smalleys' home placed a call to the Arlington apartment the girls had visited earlier that evening.

It is anyone's guess why this call was made.

Perhaps the girls were calling the boy to let it be known that they would not be returning to his apartment after all, or maybe they were calling to report their safe arrival in Carrollton. We simply do not know.

Concerning their stopover at the Smalley's home at midnight, Stacie and Susan may very well have had no intention of staying there for any length of time. Instead, the girls may have returned to Susan's house for only a short interlude because – remembering she had insisted that Stacie's midnight curfew was still in force and that they never knew when she might call – they anticipated Ida might be phoning to confirm they were actually where she wanted them to be at midnight. In this regard, said Ida, "It was the 12:01 a.m. call [to Arlington] that told me they did return to Susan's, as I had told Stacie she needed to do."[33]

It is unclear what exactly prompted Stacie and Susan to leave the comfort of the Smalley household well after midnight and venture out into the night once more. It was obviously prompted to one degree or another by simple teenage boredom, which often manifests itself in the belief that there is no such thing as having a good time at home. There is also no way of knowing, however, if the girls went out seeking something or someone in particular or if they simply went out driving around for its own sake.

In any event, once more we are left to speculate as to their whereabouts.

When I asked her if she had any inkling as to why Stacie and Susan might have gone out again that last time, Deanna Bowman Sinclair, who had almost joined Stacie and Susan on their night on the town, said:

> I do not know that there were any specific plans for that night that would have been any different than any other night...I have no idea why they would leave the house. That would be out of character for Susan and what I know of Stacie. They had to be meeting someone they knew...Susan was always careful. That is what is so puzzling. I know she would not go with someone she did not know...It had to be someone they knew to go out at that time of night.[34]

---

33 Ida Madison, June 18, 2009.
34 Deanna Bowman Sinclair, October 1, 2009.

WHEREABOUTS UNKNOWN – AN ATTEMPT TO BUY BEER?

Shortly after midnight, according to a clerk at an Addison, Texas 7-Eleven store, two girls matching Stacie's and Susan's description attempted to buy beer, despite being underage. However, because 1988 was well before the advent of reliable security cameras, the exact identities of these girls cannot be confirmed.[35]

IN THE STEAK AND ALE PARKING LOT IN ADDISON, TEXAS

After this possible stop at 7-Eleven, at some point between 12:30 a.m. and 1:30 a.m., Stacie and Susan were positively identified as being in the parking lot of the Addison Steak and Ale where Susan worked as a hostess. Insofar as anyone can tell, the girls stopped there so that, while Stacie waited in the car with the top down, Susan could visit with a "co-worker who told police that Susan had been trying to date him."[36]

WHEREABOUTS UNKNOWN – *AD INFINITUM*

Here this reconstruction ends.

Beyond this brief interlude in the Steak and Ale parking lot – with the exception of a possible sighting on Forest Lane around 1:00 a.m. – Stacie Madison and Susan Smalley have never been seen or heard from again.

For all intents and purposes, like a scene from a science fiction film, it is as if the girls slipped through a portal into another dimension. Life in what the Bible describes as a fallen world, however, reminds us that such was not the case. Instead, we know that Stacie and Susan encountered evil at some point in the wee hours of that Sunday morning.

Based upon the location where Stacie's car was later located, we can safely assume the girls parked Stacie's car in front of the baseball card shop on Forest Lane at Webbs Chapel Road, with every intention of returning to it later, and accepted a ride from persons unknown who were driving another vehicle.

Where the girls went with this person or persons and why, the extent to which they knew them, and the circumstances under which they presumably got into this person's car are the missing pieces to this puzzle.

---

35 *The Fort Worth Star-Telegram*, March 18, 1998.
36 Id.

The parking lot at Webbs Chapel Road and Forest Lane
in which Stacie Madison's 1967 Ford Mustang was located
(Photo by the author)

SHAWN SUTHERLAND

AT THE RACES ON EMERALD STREET?

It is possible the girls went to watch the races on Emerald Street in the hours after 1:00 a.m. At least two witnesses have come forward since 1988 to report they saw two "girls matching the descriptions of Susan and Stacie" at the races early that morning. According to Captain Greg Ward, these witnesses stated that these particular girls "appeared to be intoxicated and were starting the races by flashing their breasts."[37]

An alternate version of this story involves a blonde in a blue dress who was starting these races by raising her skirt. This particular story was quickly disproven by Ida Madison, who discovered Stacie's blue dress still hanging in her daughter's closet.[38]

Either way, Ida Madison and Carolyn Smalley both discount salacious stories such as these, as does Captain Ward.[39]

When I asked him if the girls in question could have been Stacie and Susan, Captain Ward told me, "There's a lot of blondes and brunettes, and from what I know about these girls, that wasn't exactly their character."[40] My opinion of such allegations, based upon what I have learned while researching this book, corresponds with those held by Carolyn, Ida, and Captain Ward.

Regardless, as with allegations that they were "party girls," whether it was Stacie and Susan baring their breasts is ultimately irrelevant.

True or not, the act of being intoxicated and the baring breasts would not have justified whatever fate befell Stacie and Susan. And to insinuate that there is any correlation or connection between the two events, or that the girls somehow brought their destinies upon themselves in any way, is an insulting manifestation of the "blame the victim" mentality.

Moreover, such lurid gossip detracts from the real issue, the real question at hand, which is what happened to Stacie Madison and Susan Smalley on the morning of Sunday, March 20, 1988?

37 *The Dallas Morning News*, August 19, 2001.
38 Ida Madison, August 3, 2009.
39 *The Dallas Morning News*, August 19, 2001.
40 Greg Ward, June 16, 2009.

115

The parking lot at Webbs Chapel Road and Forest Lane
in which Stacie Madison's 1967 Ford Mustang was located
(Photo by the author)

16

SPECULATION AND THEORIES

"The dead claim the living through imagined repetition of the horror they endured." [1]

In 2009, 21 years after the girls were last seen, what was true in 1988 is still the case today. That is, only those persons responsible for the disappearances of Stacie Madison and Susan Smalley know definitively what became of them. For everyone else, there remains only speculation.

CRAZY AND BIZARRE GUESSES

There is an old joke about everyone possessing an opinion. Unfortunately, the same cannot be said for common sense and sensitivity. Instead, some have taken the peculiar nature of the girls' disappearances as a full tilt license to run rampant with conjecture and rumor. Consequently, almost from the moment the girls were reported missing, the Carrollton Police Department's operators began fielding telephone calls from a plethora of individuals all too intent on promoting their preferred suppositions regarding what fate had befallen Stacie and Susan. Each theory logged seemed more outlandish than the previous one and seemingly included everything but Elvis Presley and the Bermuda Triangle.

Consequently, police endured an odd assortment of hypotheses, including claims that the two were abducted by aliens from outer space, spirited away to Mexico and sold into prostitution, had gone to South Padre Island to marry boyfriends, had fallen victim to a roving serial killer, were sacrificed by Satanists in honor of the Vernal Equinox, or murdered as part of an illegal organ harvesting syndicate operated by Dallas bikers and Mexican crime lords.

One individual even called police insisting that Stacie had murdered Susan in a heated argument – or maybe it was the other way around – and was now on the run from law enforcement officers. Were this true, and there is no reason whatsoever to believe it is, Stacie or Susan one deserves a medal for successfully eluding authorities for more than two decades.

---

1 James Ellroy, "The Haunting." *Newsweek*, August 10 & 17, 2009, p. 44.

EVERYBODY'S GOT A LITTLE ANGLE

When I asked Captain Greg Ward about this odd assortment of suppositions, particularly the gossip regarding the girls being transported to Mexico for forced prostitution purposes, his opinion was, "There's a lot of speculation about what happened but, in my law enforcement career, I'm not aware of anybody from the United States, the Texas area, who was abducted and sold for what they call 'White Labor.'"[2]

When presented weeks earlier with a question regarding the rampant speculation surrounding the girls' disappearances, Sergeant John Crawford had offered a similar response and added, "Everybody's got a little angle on something."[3] In other words, our television and tabloid-driven society has a tendency to reject plausible and likely explanations in favor of those which are more sensational and exotic. Of such lurid supposition, Ida Madison says, "I've heard the organ harvesting, sex slavery, kidnapped to Mexico, or other countries stories. I think the alien spaceship pickup theory is about as good as any other."[4]

HORRID THINGS

Of course, Ida does not make light of what these stories represent. "You can't possibly imagine all the scenarios I have run through my mind over the years," Ida told me, as she spoke of mental images that she described as, "horrid things, things I didn't want to imagine. They are just there, haunting me for 21 years."[5]

Out of respect for Ida, I did not ask her to elaborate on this point. Similarly, I did not ask Susan's father John Richard Smalley, for details when he said of the girls, "I've got a feeling that the worst happened to them."[6]

We are all gifted with an imagination, and it seems too many have focused on what "the worst" might have entailed and not on the fact that two girls remain missing 21 years after they vanished. In the end, speculating about such details is simply ghoulish. John Richard Smalley agrees, and says, "I figure Susan's dead. That's all there is to it."[7] I understood that Mr. Smalley meant that knowing the details of what happened to the girls would not bring his daughter back to him.

Regarding details, Carolyn Smalley says, "I have mixed emotions

---

2 Greg Ward, June 16, 2009.
3 John W. Crawford, June 4, 2009.
4 Ida Madison, August 3, 2009.
5 Id., August 10, 2009.
6 John Richard Smalley, July 5, 2009.
7 Id.

about whether I want to know for sure what happened to them."[8] In a way, she says, not knowing makes it easier to keep hope alive. Others meanwhile are determined to find out definitively what happened to Stacie Madison and Susan Smalley.

This leads us back to the question of who is responsible for the girls' disappearances

ENTIA NON SUNT MULTIPLICANDA PRAETER NECESSITATEM (ENTITIES MUST NOT BE MULTIPLIED BEYOND NECESSITY)

Sir Arthur Conan Doyle, via his creation Sherlock Holmes, once said, "As a rule, the more bizarre a thing is the less mysterious it proves to be."[9] In other words, as William of Occam first put forth in the 14th century hypothesis known as "Occam's Razor," if two or more competing theories exist to explain a given action, outcome, or event, more often than not, the theory that is the least complicated will prove to be the correct one.

In the case of Stacie and Susan, the theories in conflict are: (a) the girls were abducted completely at random and against their wills by total strangers; or (b) they willingly entered the vehicle of someone known to them who delivered them to what proved to be their final destination. Both hypotheses are possible and, accordingly, neither can be hastily dismissed.

As for the "stranger danger" scenario, it is highly unlikely, although by no means impossible, that organ thieves, pornographers, pimps, or Satanists were behind the girls' disappearances. Instead, in the "by persons unknown" equation, it is more likely that the girls were simply taken by perverted individuals with the most licentious of motives in mind. And ultimately this possibility stands or falls completely on whether it is reasonable to believe that one or more individuals could force two adult women into a vehicle against their wills at the same time on the premier cruise strip in Dallas County at an hour when, at the end of Spring Break, there would have still been a fair amount of both people and traffic out and about. Considering the cacophony and bedlam that would have most likely ensued in such a situation, Forest Lane would probably not have been the ideal spot for a seamless abduction.

Instead, on a purely contemplative level, the more rational argument is that Stacie and Susan accepted a ride on March 20, 1988 from someone they knew or otherwise trusted and that these persons are either responsible for the girls' disappearances or at minimum took

---

8 Carolyn Smalley, September 22, 2009.
9 Arthur Conan Doyle, "The Red-headed League," *The Complete Sherlock Holmes,* Volume 1, Barnes & Noble Classics, 2004, p. 215.

them to a locale where they were introduced to those individuals who are the guilty parties. As for this possibility, Ohlen Sapp, who saw Stacie Madison's Ford Mustang on the day it was recovered, told me unequivocally, "Whoever's vehicle Stacie Madison and Susan Smalley got into, they knew them."[10]

THE SOLUTION

Whether those responsible for the girls' disappearances were strangers or friends, both scenarios leave us to speculate. As well, the two theories equally illustrate just how imperative it is that those individuals with knowledge concerning the girls' fates – and someone out there unquestionably does know what became of them – finally find the courage to come forward and share what they know. This is doubly true if the parties responsible for the Stacie's and Susan's disappearances were persons known to the girls.

By any definition, the deafening silence that has persisted since March 1988 is completely unconscionable and is accordingly addressed at greater length in subsequent chapters.

---

10 Ohlen Sapp, October 17, 2009.

17

JASON LAWTON, SUSPECT

"If anything comes out of this book, Jason Lawton needs to be looked at very, very hard. He needs to be pressed. He needs to be talked to again. People do need to be interviewed on this. This idea of eliminating him because he passed a polygraph and then never talking to him again is just absurd."[1]

Perhaps the most confounding suspect the Carrollton Police Department ever considered in the disappearances of Stacie Madison and Susan Smalley was Jason Lawton, Stacie's high school boyfriend.[2]

Since his car was in the hands of either the mechanic or the repo man on the night the girls disappeared (Lawton told me two different stories on two separate occasions), he reportedly walked home from work around 11:00 p.m. after his evening shift at McDonald's ended. When I spoke with him, Lawton insisted that his brother could verify this claim.[3]

Nevertheless, and despite his statement to me that he "was never a suspect or anything," Lawton became a person of interest in the girls' disappearances after police learned that his relationship with Stacie was not only strained but that, on March 19, 1988, she was most likely at the Arlington apartment of another boy at approximately the same time Lawton was calling the Madison household in an attempt to find out where Stacie was and why she had failed to pick him up.[4]

HE IS THE ONE WHO MADE HIMSELF LOOK GUILTY

Among Ida Madison's first electronic mails to me was one in which

---

1 Ohlen Sapp, October 17, 2009.
2 The reader should note that this chapter is specifically entitled "Jason Lawton, Suspect" because Mr. Lawton has never been charged with any crime in regard to the disappearances of Stacie Madison and Susan Smalley. Accordingly, under the Amercian system of justice, he must be presumed innocent unless charged by and found guilty in a court of law. The reader need also remember that "Jason Lawton" is not this individual's true name.
3 Jason Lawton, July 15, 2009 and November 3, 2009.
4 Id., November 3, 2009.

she stated, "One theory that we have all thought of is that Jason, who called our house that night wanting Stacie, found someone to take him around looking for her and found them on Forest Lane."[5] In answer to questions regarding this possibility, Lawton reiterated that he and his brother were both without vehicles that night.[6]

When I asked Ida why she suspected Lawton, she said, "He is the one who made himself look guilty. I kept calling him [after the girls disappeared] to come get missing posters to put up, and he never would, which surprised me."[7]

Ohlen Sapp read these comments from Ida and recalled that Lawton was equally apathetic regarding the Carrollton Police Department's investigation into Stacie's and Susan's disappearances. Said Sapp of Lawton, "He did nothing to help...he had no interest in what was going on...now this is a guy who's supposed to be Stacie's boyfriend."[8]

FINDING JASON LAWTON

Having heard about Lawton from virtually the inception of this project, it was imperative that I find and interview him.

I eventually located Lawton and his fourth wife in one of the Upland South states where he lives in a community of approximately 5,000 people under a surname other than the one with which he graduated from Newman Smith High School.

Over the course of a week in July 2009, I twice telephoned what turned out to be Lawton's home. Both times I left messages, once on his answering machine and another time with an individual who seemed rather stunned by my questions.

Eventually returning my call from a mobile phone, Lawton reluctantly agreed to speak with me. His reason for so doing, he said, was that he knew that refusing to do so would make him appear guilty in the eyes of readers.[9]

"I FELT SO ALIENATED"

Lawton's decision to return my call no doubt stems from his first hand knowledge of what it means to be presumed guilty by others. This he presumably learned in 1988 courtesy of the Carrollton Police Department.

---

5 Ida Madison, June 18, 2009.
6 Jason Lawton, November 3, 2009.
7 Ida Madison, July 16, 2009.
8 Ohlen Sapp, October 17, 2009.
9 Jason Lawton, July 15, 2009.

"Cops came around every day," Lawton said, as he recalled the frequency with which the police questioned him in the months after Stacie and Susan vanished. "They kept coming to my job repeatedly."[10]

It is a matter of dispute as to whether police actually visited Lawton during his shifts at work, but Lawton insists that such was the case and that this "outside interference" cost him both his job at McDonald's and a subsequent one at Burger King.

The attention also cost Lawton numerous friendships.

"I felt so alienated," Lawton lamented when I asked him to speak about Stacie's and Susan's disappearances.[11] "I had nothing to do with it," he swore to me. Still people who had known him all his life quickly began asking him if he knew anything about the girls' fates, if not accusing him outright. These people, as well as police, were not entirely without their reasons.

A STRONG SUSPECT

On the day that I interviewed him, former Carrollton police investigator David Bock had traveled from Houston to Dallas to meet with me. One of the first things he said was, "The reason I'm here is because you hadn't heard how strong of a suspect Lawton was...he had motive, means and opportunity."[12] Lawton had also offered the world another reason to suspect him – a confession.

AN IMPROMPTU CONFESSION

Prior to meeting with Sapp and Bock, I had read a 1998 article from *The Fort Worth Star-Telegram* recounting how, a decade earlier, Lawton had impulsively confessed to his girlfriend that he had bludgeoned Stacie and Susan both and buried their bodies in a local cemetery. According to that article, Lawton, when interrogated by police, insisted that he made this reckless statement in the heat of a thoughtless moment because he had grown "exasperated with people asking him about Stacie's disappearance and implying that he knew something about it."[13] The actual story, however, is far more complicated.

---

10 Id.
11 Jason Lawton, July 15, 2009.
12 David Bock, October 17, 2009.
13 *The Fort Worth Star-Telegram*, March 18, 1998.

HUMAN NATURE IS HUMAN NATURE

In October 2009, I was eventually able to sit down with David Bock and Ohlen Sapp, the original investigators in the Madison/Smalley case, and discuss Lawton's confession and the investigation it spawned. This was a moment I had awaited for quite some time. Apparently, Sapp and Bock had been equally anxious to discuss this point.

Settling in to offer me his recollections regarding Lawton's bizarre declaration, Bock prefaced them with the preamble:

> Not 90 days after the disappearance of these two girls, who haven't been found yet, Lawton has already moved on and now he's got another girlfriend...human nature is human nature...how unusual is it for someone to move on with a new girlfriend in three months when the old girlfriend is still missing?[14]

LAWTON'S CONFESSION

I shall hereafter refer to the woman Lawton was dating during the summer of 1988 as "Dena Sayed," although this is not her real name.

Continuing with his narrative, Bock related how, in June 1988, Ms. Sayed appeared at the Carrollton police station with her mother and offered that she and Lawton had been in his car just days earlier when:

> Lawton makes a statement to the effect of "I feel bad" or "It's a shame that Mrs. Madison is still looking for Stacie." That has a lot of credibility with the way that came out. The girl asks for some details. Lawton hesitates, and then he says that he met them, picked them up down on Forest Lane, took them in his car up to a cemetery, hit them in the head with a shovel and buried their bodies. Very specific. She says, "Where did that happen?" They were driving down Highway 121 eastbound. He points out the window and says 'Up there."[15]

THE STORY REPEATED

Another person to hear Lawton's story was Ida Madison, who interviewed Ms. Sayed shortly after the latter's interview with police. At their meeting, Ida took notes regarding what Ms. Sayed said.

---

14 David Bock, October 17, 2009.
15 Id.

According to these notes:

> Dena Sayed said she and Jason were at Furneaux Theater one night and Jason said Stacie "looked like a chicken with her head cut off" after he hit her over the head with a shovel. Dena asked what he was talking about. He said he hit Stacie and Susan over the head with a shovel and buried them in a cemetery.
>
> I asked Dena if she had asked Jason if he had anything to do with Stacie's and Susan's disappearance. Dena said she had not asked Jason that because she thought he was upset about Stacie.
>
> Dena told Jason to let her out of the car, and she was going to tell the police. Jason said he would kill Dena if she went to the police. Dena said Neal Lawton [Jason's brother] was Jason's alibi for the night...Dena said she was at the police station from 10:00 p.m. until 3:00 a.m.[16]

LAWTON'S VERSION OF EVENTS

When I spoke with him in November 2009, following my interview with Sapp and Bock, Lawton offered his own recollection of the event.

What Lawton recalled was that he and Ms. Sayed were returning a video to a local rental store when Ms. Sayed reportedly asked Lawton if he had been involved in Stacie's and Susan's disappearances. This question, according to Lawton, hurt his feelings and provoked him to then say that he had bludgeoned the girls and dumped their bodies inside the fish hatchery on Highway 121. He stated that he had mentioned the fish hatchery to Sayed because he had once gone there with friends and because it was a locale that was "out of the way." When pressed for a reason as to why he would do something so asinine as to make such a claim if it were not true, Lawton offered that he wanted Ms. Sayed to know what it was like to be afraid, if only for a short while. This, he said, was so that she might understand what his life was like since everyone was now presuming he had something to do with Stacie's and Susan's disappearances.[17]

---

16 Ida Madison, October 18, 2009. Please note that "Dena Sayed" and "Neal Lawton" are not these individuals' true names.
17 Jason Lawton, November 3, 2009.

A HIDDEN CEMETERY

In reflecting upon these conflicting versions of events, I recalled how weeks earlier David Bock had stated, "If Lawton was making a confession to his girlfriend, part could be true, part could not be...if [Stacie's and Susan's bodies are] not at that cemetery, I don't think that discredits the whole story."[18] I also recalled how Bock stated that he had interviewed Ms. Sayed personally and believed she "had a great deal of credibility."[19]

As demonstrated by their subsequent actions, Sapp and Bock both obviously shared this same opinion. Case in point, the day after she was interviewed by Bock, the two detectives together took Ms. Sayed for a car ride that led them east on Highway 121. There they requested that Ms. Sayed identify the spot to which Lawton had pointed when making what Bock referred to as a "statement against self interest."[20] After noting the area the girl had indicated, the investigators then dropped her off and went on a scouting expedition of their own. Returning to the location Ms. Sayed had identified (i.e., Highway 121 and Fish Hatchery Road), the two investigators discovered precisely what Jason Lawton had described – an isolated, private cemetery unknown to the general public.[21]

Given that the detective's discovery correlated so strongly with the story Ms. Sayed said Lawton had relayed to her, the two officers requested permission to search this cemetery.

Officers from the Carrollton Police Department did venture to the cemetery, and even scouted the surrounding area extensively, but found no recently disturbed ground or anything else to suggest that a more extensive search (e.g., one involving cadaver dogs or a ground stripping) was in order.[22]

A PRACTICED LIAR?

Confronted with and interrogated by Sapp and Bock about Sayed's revelations and the discovery of the cemetery, Lawton agreed to

18 Id.
19 David Bock, October 17, 2009.
20 Id.
21 Out of respect for the surviving members of the family for whom this cemetery is named, especially considering that it has been senselessly vandalized in recent years, the cemetery's name is intentionally not included here. Additionally, curiosity seekers wishing to venture to this cemetery are cautioned to note that the cemetery is now surrounded by government land overseen by the U.S. Army Corps of Engineers, who removed the Fish Hatchery Road Bridge leading to the cemetery in the early 2000s. Consequently, given the combined security precautions put in place by the family and the U.S. Army Corps of Engineers, unfettered access to the cemetery is impossible.
22 Joel Payne, November 3, 2009.

submit to a polygraph test. Lawton, it must be noted, passed this examination.

Ida Madison was not impressed. "He passed," she says. "However, that wouldn't be difficult for a practiced liar, as I had learned he was."[23]

In a similar vein, David Bock, when reflecting on the fact that Lawton passed the test, posed the rhetorical question:

> Do [polygraph tests] say whether the person is lying or not? Absolutely not. What a polygraph shows is a reaction to a question. Some people, sociopaths, for example, may not have the same reaction that you or I, who have a strong sense of conscience, would.[24]

Likewise, Carolyn Smalley told me:

> I didn't really know Stacie's boyfriend, but I knew he was a liar right from the beginning. He told the police [when the girls first disappeared that] he didn't know where Susan lived, but I came home one night and he was knocking on my front door because Stacie was over there.[25]

Carolyn also added that she likewise later heard stories in which it was alleged, but unsubstantiated, that Lawton had "pulled knives on people at parties [and] was violent and apt to do something."[26]

Regardless, since Lawton had passed the polygraph test, the Carrollton Police Department was presumably of the opinion that it lacked the legal right and lacked sufficient grounds to continue with any further interrogation of Lawton.

A DEPARTURE FROM TEXAS

Lawton was now no longer a suspect in the disappearances of Stacie Madison and Susan Smalley. However, being in a position where he says he "had nothing left" in Texas (i.e., no job, no prospects and no friends), within weeks of passing the polygraph test, he moved to a state in the Deep South.[27] There, he legally changed his last name to that of the biological father he had never known but with whom he reconnected. In this state, he also married four times. The

23 Ida Madison, June 9, 2009.
24 David Bock, October 17, 2009.
25 Carolyn Smalley, July 14, 2009.
26 Id.
27 Jason Lawton, November 3, 2009

end result was that, as he did his best to move on with his life, Lawton was all but forgotten by the Carrollton Police Department. Yet not everyone forgot.

LAWTON'S EX-MOTHER-IN-LAW

Years later, Ida told me, she hoped Carrollton police would reconsider and reexamine Lawton as a suspect. That was in the early 1990s when Lawton's then mother-in-law, a woman whom I shall refer to here as "Avis Morgan," contacted both Ida and Carrollton police.[28] Morgan had felt compelled to call from another state because she could no longer abide Lawton physically abusing her daughter. By means unknown, Morgan had learned of Stacie Madison's and Susan Smalley's disappearances and questioned what Lawton's involvement may have been. Thus, she telephoned small towns in Texas until she hit upon the one wherein Lawton had been suspected in the disappearances of two girls whose whereabouts remained unknown. Having spoken with the Carrollton Police Department, Morgan then telephoned Ida Madison. Her point in calling Carrollton police, she told Ida, was a simple desire to alert someone in Texas to what she perceived to be a pattern of abuse on Lawton's part. She was also hoping, she later confessed, to have Lawton extradited to Texas if for no other reason than to permanently remove him from her daughter's life.[29]

AN ABUSIVE HUSBAND?

I spoke with Avis Morgan over the telephone on numerous occasions while writing this book and her stories about Lawton physically abusing her daughter never wavered. One instance, of Lawton's violent nature, she said, allegedly involved him slamming her daughter's head against a fireplace.[30]

When confronted with these accusations of abuse, Lawton told me, "That's hard to explain. You'd have to know my ex-wife." After making this statement, he related how his ex-wife was 17 years old when, at 24 years of age, he had married her. His ex-wife, Lawton insisted, was the violent one in their relationship, that she often pulled knives on him, and that any physical confrontations he had with her were simply for his own self-protection. In fact, he asserted, Avis Morgan

---

28 Claiming that she has endeavored to remake her life since their divorce, and given her fear of reprisals from him, Lawton's ex-wife declined all requests for an interview. As well, Lawton's ex-mother-in-law agreed to speak with me only on the condition that I not use her true name. She is, therefore, referred to here as "Avis Morgan."
29 Ida Madison, June 20, 2009.
30 Avis Morgan, September 29, 2009 and October 13, 2009.

sanctioned the marriage in order to get her violence prone daughter out of her house. He then posed a rhetorical question in which he asked me, if indeed he is so violent, why does one of his other ex-wives have no problem with allowing him to take custody of their daughter during the summer? "I'm not abusive," Lawton insisted.[31]

I re-interviewed Avis Morgan following my final conversation with Jason Lawton. She challenged his recollections and said that, should anyone care to research the subject, a restraining order had been sought against Lawton for a very specific reason and that a paper trail existed documenting the specific details as to why.[32]

QUESTIONS AND RESERVATIONS

Said Ida of these allegations of abuse against Lawton:

> I really didn't think early on that Jason would have hurt Stacie. After I heard Jason had hit Stacie, though, and especially after I heard from Jason's mother-in-law, I believed he was capable of it.[33]

The reader must recognize that being capable of something is not necessarily the same thing as being guilty. However, Ida Madison unequivocally declares she has questions and reservations about Lawton she wishes police would explore.

Ohlen Sapp and David Bock also wish that the Carrollton Police Department would reexamine Jason Lawton. In this regard, David Bock said:

> I think it's ludicrous that, after 22 years, it's still an open investigation, and [the Carrollton Police Department is] saying it's just a missing person case...that's ludicrous...a fresh look needs to be taken at this case, and in particular Jason Lawton...if you can eliminate Lawton, great. But I don't think it's been done yet.[34]

Sapp agreed, saying:

> This whole decision to eliminate Lawton as a suspect was based on a polygraph test...if anything comes out of this book, Jason Lawton needs to be looked at very, very hard. He

---

31 Jason Lawton, November 3, 2009.
32 Avis Morgan, November 4, 2009.
33 Ida Madison, July 16, 2009.
34 David Bock, October 17, 2009.

needs to be pressed. Lawton needs to be talked to again. People do need to be interviewed on this. This idea of eliminating Lawton because he passed a polygraph and then never talking to him again is just absurd...he had a motive. Lawton had the opportunity...this case deserves for every lead to be exhausted...Lawton was not ever properly eliminated as a suspect in the case.

Concerning Sapp's and Bock's respective statements, the reader should note two things. Regarding the classification of the case, on the same day that I spoke with Lawton for the second time, a representative of the Carrollton Police Department explained to me that the department has chosen to label the investigation a missing persons case all these years because, whenever physical remains are located throughout the country, they are immediately compared with the databases regarding open missing persons cases. (On this subject, Sergeant John Crawford said, "DNA samples from both mothers were added to the Combined DNA Index System, making it possible to match any remains that might be found in the U.S."[35]) To reclassify the case as a homicide, then, would be to remove Stacie Madison and Susan Smalley from those databases. That would mean the girls' remains might never be identified. Moreover, this same peace officer assured me that Lawton has never been eliminated as a suspect in the case. In fact, he said, when it comes to the Madison/Smalley case, "There have been very, very few outright eliminations".[36]

GOSSIP ON FOREST LANE

All of this aside, one thing is certain: gossip regarding Lawton's role in the girls' disappearances is alive and well in Dallas, Texas.

After I decided to undertake this project, word spread quickly that I was writing a book about the disappearances of Stacie Madison and Susan Smalley. Ironically, as I began editing an early draft of this chapter, I received an email from an individual whom I will identify as "Adam Byrd." Recalling 1988, he said:

> I was just beginning to go out to Forest Lane, but I remember hearing what had happened...I do remember two brothers with the last name "Lawton" living in Carrollton that supposedly knew what happened. I'm a little hesitant to say, but I remember one of them, "Neal Lawton," to be a little crazy

---

35 John Crawford, October 20, 2009.
36 Joel Payne, November 3, 2009.

compared to your average teenager...I heard back then that supposedly one or both of the girls had been buried in or near the old cemetery off of Fish Hatchery Road and Highway 121...people used to go out there to party and shoot guns, etc...you would be surprised how old and remote it is.[37]

I discussed the specifics of this gossip with Ohlen Sapp and David Bock on the day that I met with them. They thought that what "Adam Byrd" shared was intriguing and noteworthy. This eventually led Ohlen Sapp to offer that Jason Lawton should bear in mind that, "There are people on this planet that think the proper person was identified...there are people on this planet that think he [Jason Lawton] did it, and I'm one of them." In response, David Bock quickly interjected, "I'm one of them too."[38]

I discussed this gossip with Jason Lawton himself. In regard to such rumors, Lawton informed me, in no uncertain terms, "I'm not responsible and my brother couldn't be...neither one of us had anything to do with it." Lawton then offered that his brother is learning disabled and was, in fact, unable to do basic things such as count change until he was in his 20s. Lawton likewise stated the allegation was "not in the realm of reality." He then notified me that:

I wish they would find whoever did it so my life could go to normal...someone I knew disappeared and I had nothing to do with it...I answered all [your] questions, basically, because they have nothing to do with Stacie and Susan but with how I live my life...it's all just crap...I was allowed to leave Carrollton...I'm not trying to be nasty towards you, but it's 20 years later and I'm still answering the same questions...it's affected my life also in a way that no one ever thinks of..I never was a suspect.[39]

WHAT IS THE ANSWER?

So, is Lawton guilty of murder? I do not know. I was not with Stacie Madison and Susan Smalley on the night they disappeared nor am I psychic.

I do know that I am troubled by the confession Jason Lawton offered Dena Sayed, especially when it is coupled with the allegations that he physically abused both Stacie Madison and at least one of his

---

37 "Adam Byrd," August 19, 2009 and September 15, 2009. Please note that neither "Adam Byrd" nor "Neal Lawton" are these individual's' true names.
38 David Bock and Ohlen Sapp, October 17,2009.
39 Jason Lawton, November 3, 2009.

ex-wives. I am also disturbed by Lawton's abrupt exodus to another state so quickly after passing the polygraph test when, despite his claims that he had no hope of finding a job in Dallas, his adoptive father (whose name Lawton bore until 1990) owned a chain of retail stores in the Dallas/Fort Worth Metroplex area.

Recent history, in the person of Carl Probyn, Jaycee Lee Dugard's step-father, demonstrates that people can be wrong in their assumptions. Specifically, until Dugard was recently discovered alive, Probyn had for years been adjudged guilty in the eyes of many of masterminding his step-daughter's 1991 disappearance. The differences between Probyn and Lawton, however, cannot be overlooked. For one thing, unlike Lawton, at no time did Probyn ever confess to murdering Dugard regardless of his circumstances. As well, Probyn was never accused of committing a criminal offense (i.e., physically abusing a spouse a la Lawton) that echoes by degree the subject matter of another crime in which he was suspected (i.e., Lawton and the deaths of Stacie Madison and Susan Smalley).

Therefore, I must admit that I would rest easier if, as Sapp and Bock insist should be the case, those close to Lawton (e.g., his family, friends and ex-wives, et al.) were pressed in order to determine what Lawton has said to others since March 1988 in regard to the disappearances of Stacie Madison and Susan Smalley. As well, given that the story he told in 1988 about burying the girls in a cemetery conflicts with the story he told me in 2009 about dumping them in the fish hatchery, there may be aspects of Lawton's stories that the Carrollton Police Department have not yet investigated. It might behoove all concerned, including Lawton, to explore all possibilities once and for all. After all, if Lawton is innocent, exhausting this lead might offer him the closure he maintains he wants.

Ultimately, time alone will tell what avenues the Carrollton Police Department will explore in regard to the girls' disappearances and what long silenced answers remain to be discovered.

Chapters of this story definitely remain to be written. Stacie Madison and Susan Smalley deserve no less.

18

AFTERSHOCKS

"The dead claim the living...through the imposition of grief...This is the living telling the dead how much they are loved and how irretrievable the loss of them is." [1]

Since Stacie Madison and Susan Smalley were last seen in March 1988, the landscape of the world has changed considerably.

At the time of the girls' disappearances, Ronald Reagan was in the last months of his historic Presidency. Names on the music charts that year included Taylor Dayne, Guns N' Roses, Whitney Houston, INXS, George Michael, Robert Palmer, Pet Shop Boys, and Steve Winwood.

Among the most popular films of 1988 – many of which were released after March 1988 – were *Beaches*, *Big*, *Die Hard*, *The Naked Gun*, *Rain Man*, *Who Framed Roger Rabbit*, *Willow*, and *Young Guns*.

Stacie and Susan would no doubt be shocked by the world of 2009. They would be equally overwhelmed to discover the extent to which their disappearances have impacted not just family and friends, but their classmates and community as well. They might not understand it, but they would be unable to deny the way their disappearances have impacted the lives of others. This was true virtually from day one.

SOMBER AND SURREAL

Almost immediately, the events of March 20, 1988 sent tremors through the student body and faculty at Newman Smith High School. The aftershocks pulsate to this day.

Robin Hohner Devenish, then a student at Smith, said, "Stacie and I knew each other because she had kind of dated a friend of mine. I remember being so shocked when they went missing." [2]

Devenish is not alone.

Stacey Allmon Simpson is among those with whom I spoke who described the mood of the Newman Smith High School student body as somber following the disappearances

---

1 James Ellroy, "The Haunting," *Newsweek*, August 10 & 17, 2009, p. 44.
2 Robin Hohner Devenish, January 25, 2009.

"For a long time, we kept thinking they would show up. Then we kept thinking there would at least be an explanation."[3]

"When such was not forthcoming," says Devenish, "the resulting feeling was surreal."[4]

Toni McNamara Wylie was friends with both girls; Susan was her neighbor and she shared a vocational education class with Stacie. "It was just so odd," she said. "These two girls were intelligent and seemed to stay out of trouble."[5]

A CLOUD OVER THE CAMPUS

The emotional confusion was not reserved for the student body alone.

"The whole situation of two girls just disappearing at that time was not real," said Jon Bohls, former Head Band Director at Smith. "That just didn't happen – then or now".[6]

Bohls' fellow faculty member, C. Kenneth Dockray, Smith's Director of Orchestral Activities for many years, remembers there was a "great deal of sadness and concern about how they disappeared and why they weren't found."[7]

Joe Pouncy, who was a teacher at Smith in 1988 and is today the school's principal, told me it was "as if a cloud had descended over the campus." He added that, for those teachers who were at Smith in 1988, it is a cloud that lingers. "It's just one of those unresolved things," Pouncy said.[8]

FOREST LANE AFFECTED

In May 1988, two months after the girls disappeared, Dr. Charles Blanton, the school's principal, was quoted in the *The Dallas Morning News* as saying that students at Smith had gone "from mad, to wondering where [Stacie and Susan] are, to caution, to fear. Some of them have said, 'That could happen to me.'"[9]

As Susan's friend Deanna Bowman Sinclair, put it, "If this can happen to Susan, it can happen to anyone. What is really frightening is that Stacie and Susan were together."[10]

These emotions poured out from the Smith student body and in

3 Paul Joseph Smith, September 4, 2009.
4 Stacey Allmon Simpson, June 8, 2009.
5 Toni McNamara Wylie, February 27, 2009.
6 Jon Bohls, July 17, 2009.
7 C. Kenneth Dockray, July 26, 2009.
8 Joe Pouncy, September 18, 2009.
9 *The Dallas Morning News*, May 15, 1988.
10 Deanna Bowman Sinclair, October 1, 2009.

time flooded into and affected areas far beyond the school.

"I was in the R.L. Turner Class of 1988," Helga Dannheim Lewenberg told me. "I remember the whole Stacie and Susan abduction well."

The incident altered Lewenberg's life in that, like numerous others, it opened her eyes to the reality that all too often trust was thoughtlessly dispensed on Forest Lane. She said:

> I used to have friends drop me off on Forest, and I would hitch rides there with people for fun, until I came across someone I knew to take me home. After that incident, though, I never did that again.[11]

Lewenberg is but one of the many people who told me that, with Stacie's and Susan's disappearances, their days of cruising Forest Lane ended with an abrupt and screeching halt.

Granted, I also encountered a good many people who cruised Forest Lane post-1988 that had never even heard of Stacie Madison, Susan Smalley or of their abduction.

This is despite the press attention the case received for years.

PRESS COVERAGE

Newspapers revisited the case nearly every year between 1989 and 1998 on the anniversaries of the girls' disappearances. The story also appeared on the syndicated television programs *Crimestoppers 800* and *Missing...Reward* in the early 1990s. (Ida Madison reports that a woman Lawton was dating during this period later notified her that she watched one of these programs with Lawton when it was broadcast and that something about it elicited from Lawton a near hysterical reaction.[12]) As well, Stacie Madison's photograph was displayed on an episode of *The Oprah Winfrey Show* in the early 1990s regarding missing and abducted children. Her photo was displayed again in October 2009, during the episode featuring Jaycee Dugard.

For the people who missed these stories, the party on Forest Lane, as well as life in general, continued uninterrupted.

For others, the grave overtone of the entire event was not easily overcome.

---

11 Helga Dannheim Lewenberg, June 10, 2009.
12 Ida Madison, June 20, 2009 .

PSYCHOLOGICAL FALLOUT

One friend of Susan's whom I interviewed for this book – and whom I shall refer to here as "Brenda" – informed me that the incomprehensibility of two people she knew completely disappearing from the face of the Earth without a trace instilled in her such an overwhelming sense of bewilderment that she required counseling with a psychologist in order to move beyond the emotional fallout from the event. For others, this disorientation has never really subsided.

Of her daughter's disappearance, Ida Madison says, "This horrendous crime is something that has affected every facet of my family's life."[13] This has manifested itself in any number of ways. In May 1988, for example, the Madison family felt compelled to leave town the weekend of what would have been Stacie's and Susan's high school graduation. The reason, says Ida, was her feeling that:

> Our presence, I think, would have cast a pall over what should have been a happy occasion for all those other kids. I just didn't want to do that. Dr. Blanton, the principal at Newman Smith High School in 1988, brought me Stacie's cap and gown, and he brought me her diploma before graduation.[14]

These items sat on the dresser in Stacie's bedroom for months after they were delivered.[15] Eventually, the cap and gown were stored away, but it was a painful event, especially for Stacie's father.[16]

Also bittersweet were the calls of encouragement from the girls' friends which came in the months after the girls disappeared. For the most part, these calls "dwindled away" as those friends relocated to various colleges and moved on with their own lives.[17]

Stacie's and Susan's families also attempted to go on with their lives.

CARRYING ON

But just how does one carry on in the face of such a tragic event? I posed this question to both Ida Madison and Carolyn Smalley.

Ida Madison said she found the resolve to go on with life in the days immediately following the girls' disappearances because, she says:

13 Ida Madison, August 19, 2009.
14 Id., June 20, 2009.
15 *The Dallas Morning News*, May 15, 1988.
16 Kathy Jackson, "Leads are few a year after teens vanished," *The Dallas Morning News*, March 20, 1989 and Ida Madison, June 20, 2009.
17 *The Dallas Morning News*, March 20, 1988

I realized very quickly that the world did not stop revolving just because my daughter disappeared. I had two other daughters, and I couldn't let them stay in that place. And I had to be supportive of my husband because he had a really hard time.[18]

So, Ida kept her grief to herself and, when she felt overwhelmed by sorrow and discouragement, she tried to find quiet time for herself. It was in these moments of solitude that she would allow herself to cry.[19]

IDA – RELYING ON FAITH

In these instances, Ida would also turn to God. She has always had a resolute Christian faith and said of this in 2001:

I've always had a really strong belief in God. One of the things the Bible tells us is that God will never give us more than we can handle. I've tried to take things day by day. If I can get through today, I tell myself, then I can get through tomorrow. But, yes, it's a nightmare, one of those dreams that never seems to end. I keep thinking I'll wake up, but I haven't. I'm still in the nightmare. It's still going on. And it probably always will be.[20]

When I interviewed her, I asked Ida to expound on this statement. Her response was, "I have a very strong faith in God. I just know that, whatever happens, God is looking out for Stacie and for us."[21]

CAROLYN – ACCENTUATING THE POSITIVE

I would also ask Carolyn Smalley how she had found the strength to go forward.

On the day that I met with her, I knew that Carolyn had told the press in 1988 that she had dealt with Susan's disappearance initially by "involving herself in her work at a local insurance agency" and by going "out with friends to help pass the time." She had also said, "You've got to go on and do things. You can't just sit in your house and wait. And being out and being with people makes it easier to deal

---

18 Ida Madison, June 20, 2009.
19 Id., June 20, 2009.
20 *The Dallas Morning News*, August 19, 2001.
21 Ida Madison, June 20, 2009.

with."[22]

But how does she keep herself moving today? She is, after all, now separated from 1988 by a span of 21 years.

In response to this query, Carolyn told me, in a statement that suggested that perhaps she believed March 20, 1988 was part of Susan's inescapable destiny, "I do believe that if it's our time to leave this world, it will happen to us no matter where we are, and this belief has kept me going."[23]

She said she also keeps going by accentuating the positives in her life:

> As difficult as this is to handle, you have to look on the good side...I had Susan for 18 and a half years. There's a lot of people I know who have their children for three months and then they die...I always have felt lucky to have had two very good, responsible, happy kids who went to school every day, made good grades and were willing to work for their goals...I've still got Richard, and now he's got the three kids.[24]

Among Rich's children, Carolyn's grandchildren, is a daughter who not only bears the middle name of the aunt she never knew but in whom Rich says he occasionally sees hints of a personality very much like that of his sister Susan.[25]

PERSONAL FOR POLICE OFFICERS

The families are not the only ones who are regularly reminded of Stacie and Susan.

For authorities, who have uncovered little in the 21 years since the girls vanished, the case remains a source of dissatisfaction. When I interviewed him, Sergeant John Crawford told me that, as a police officer, you cannot let your cases haunt you. Yet, despite this admonition, Captain Greg Ward said, "What's frustrating for me is that I've got two mothers out there who don't know. And you talk to an Ida everyday for however-long-it-was...it is frustrating...it becomes personal...you do feel like you know them [Stacie and Susan] very well and you get to know their families."[26]

---

22 *The Dallas Morning News*, May 15, 1988.
23 Carolyn Smalley, September 22, 2009.
24 Carolyn Smalley, July 14, 2009 and September 22, 2009.
25 Rich Smalley, June 27, 2009.
26 Greg Ward, June 16, 2009.

PERSONAL FOR FRIENDS

The girls' disappearances are personal for many others as well.

Toni McNamara Wylie says of Stacie and Susan, "I have never stopped thinking about them."[27]

Laurie Lillback Gage, who grew up with Stacie, keeps her childhood friend's graduation portrait in a frame in her home. This is because, Gage says, "She will always hold a special place in my heart."[28]

Heidi Monk Wilhelm, who was probably Stacie's closest friend, recalls the girl she literally knew since infancy with the following words:

> Stacie is like a sister to me. I can't describe the void that is in my heart and in my life. I miss her! We grew up together. The memories are countless. We shared a lot of laughter, some tears, fears, and, of course, secrets. Stacie is and will always be a very special part of my life.[29]

Joe Pouncy, the current principal at Newman Smith High School, told me, "These young ladies have been in my prayers for over twenty years."[30]

Likewise, Crystal Rainwater-Roberson considers the Madison and Smalley families who stand in the shadow of this mysterious event. "My prayers go out to Susan's mother and her brother and to Stacie's family," she told me.[31]

Michelle Rohne, also a friend of both girls, said, "I hope this book will show people these girls are more than just an unsolved case or a statistic. They were and are still loved and missed very much."[32]

THE PAST MOLDING THE FUTURE

For others, the girls' disappearances have shaped their relationships with members of their own families.

Stacie's boyfriend, Greg Batchelor, told me:

> My older sister, Dawn, and I talk about Stacie frequently. All of my family loved Stacie. It was hard not to. They all treated her like family, and her family treated me the same. My sister, Dawn, was living in Virginia Beach after Stacie's

---

27 Toni McNamara Wylie, February 27, 2009
28 Laurie Lillback Gage, June 9, 2009.
29 Heidi Monk Wilhelm, August 11, 2009.
30 Joe Pouncy, June 15, 2009.
31 Crystal Rainwater-Roberson, June 2, 2009.
32 Michelle Rohne, August 25, 2009.

disappearance. While living there, she came across a milk carton with Stacie's picture on it. This has always stayed with Dawn, and kind of makes her feel part of it.[33]

For others, such as Marisa Barrier, who recalls Stacie as a girl with whom she often shared a smile and a laugh in the hallways of Newman Smith High School, remembering alone was not enough. In January 2009, she began a Facebook group entitled "Never Forget Stacie Madison and Susan Smalley."

When asked why she took it upon herself to create such a website, Marisa stated:

> I have always felt helpless when thinking about what happened to them. Starting a Facebook group was something I could do to help preserve their memory and to contribute to the effort to find them...As long as people remember them, there's still a chance that they can be found.[34]

Most fulfilling about creating the group, says Marisa, is that within minutes of its creation someone who knew Stacie and Susan joined the group. "I think this speaks volumes," she says, "on how much Susan and Stacie are on the minds and in the hearts of their classmates."[35]

Andrew Jayroe is evidence of this truth. He stated at Marisa's group, "I drive down Forest Lane about once a week these days, and I think about Stacie and Susan often."[36]

Joe Pouncy, too, thinks of the girls. "Susan and Stacie were students in my social studies class in 1988," Pouncy told me. "The disappearance of these two great young ladies was tragic and disturbing to the Newman Smith community in 1988, and remains tragic and disturbing to us in 2009."[37]

Paul Joseph Smith, who knew both girls and was a student at Smith in 1988, said that he often recalls their story today to remind himself that the ultimate reason the girls disappeared is that we live in a fallen world ruled by a malevolent entity, Satan, whose objective is to destroy the lives of God's children. When I spoke with him, Smith added that the mystery of Stacie's and Susan's disappearances will only be solved through the power of prayer.[38]

Some, such as veteran teacher Robert Hembree, believe

---

33 Greg Batchelor, August 19, 2009.
34 Marisa Barrier, July 9, 2009.
35 Id.
36 Andrew Jayroe, January24, 2009.
37 Joe Pouncy, June 15, 2009.
38 Paul Joseph Smith, September 4, 2009.

accentuating the tragic nature of the girls' disappearances can be a productive exercise, a means of avoiding similar tragedies in the future. "I will mention it nearly every year in some form or fashion just to make the kids aware of the world we live in," he says.[39]

Others also look for ways to raise awareness.

YOU NEVER KNOW WHEN IT MIGHT HAPPEN TO YOU

As I was writing this chapter, I learned that Stefanie Madison, Stacie's sister who was six years old in 1988, was organizing a child safety seminar for parents in the apartment complex in which she lives. The keynote speaker was to be none other than Captain Greg Ward.

Ida Madison, too, regularly delivers public addresses concerning missing and exploited children. What she stresses, she says, is that parents need to get involved in their children's lives, take the time to get to know their children, their activities and their children's friends, so that "if something happens, you know where to start looking.[40]

IT'S ALWAYS THERE

Such exercises are no doubt therapeutic by degree. In the end, though, they can offer only limited healing. They cannot bring back what is lost or remove an ache that will not dissipate. Nothing can do this. Nothing will. The girls' loved ones who do not speak in public know this just as well as those who do. As John Richard Smalley, Susan's father, told me in his stoic manner, "Life goes on. You learn to live with it, but it's always there."[41]

---

39 Robert Hembree, August 12, 2009.
40 Ida Madison, June 20, 2009.
41 John Richard Smalley, July 5, 2009.

THIS TREE IS
DEDICATED TO
NEWMAN SMITH
STUDENTS

STACIE ELISABETH
MADISON
AND
SUSAN RENEE
SMALLEY

DISAPPEARED
MARCH 19
1988

Memorial to the girls erected in front of Newman Smith High School
(Photo by the author)

19

THE TIME IS NOW

It is now time for someone to finally do the right thing and share what they know about the murders of Stacie Madison and Susan Smalley.

As I write this chapter, Stacie Madison and Susan Smalley have been missing from the world that knew them for nearly 22 years.

The girls are not just missing.   They are also presumed dead.   Such has been the case for quite some time now.   In the case of Stacie Madison, as mentioned previously, she was declared legally dead at the time that her father's estate was probated in 1996.

TROUBLESOME WORDS

I have avoided speaking in such terms as "death" and "murder" until now when discussing the events of March 20, 1988 because, knowing the Madison and Smalley families will read this book, I have done my best to be sensitive to their feelings.

This chapter, though, is about how it is now time for people who know something about the girls' deaths to finally speak up regarding what they know about this case.   In other words, since it is lost on some people anyway, the time for subtlety is over.   And it is now time for someone to finally do the right thing and share what they know about the murders of Stacie Madison and Susan Smalley.

GOOD AT KEEPING SECRETS

One certainty in all of this is that whoever is responsible for Stacie's and Susan's deaths is talented at keeping secrets.

I offer this observation knowing that crimes are often solved owing to humankinds' common inability to keep its collective mouth shut.   Case in point, everyone has heard of at least one murderer who was captured because, in either a moment of confession or braggadocio, they shared the details of their crime with a person who was equally incapable of keeping mum.   Thus far, though, the mystery of the girls' deaths is one surrounded by silence.

So where are these silent individuals responsible for the murders of two innocent girls?   Are they still in society, walking among us, raising families of their own, and living ordinary lives?

EVEN IF MY DAUGHTER IS DEAD...

As does everyone familiar with it, I pray that justice will be delivered to the Madison and Smalley families.

I pray also that the persons responsible for Stacie's and Susan's deaths are haunted by their crime in their dreams each night. I am sure, though, that this is not the case. Instead, since these individuals are apparently sociopaths without soul or conscience, they probably sleep just fine. That is the ultimate injustice.

James Ellroy, the author of such mystery novels as *L.A. Confidential*, has said, "It's my emphatic assertion that 'closure' is a fatuous notion that no secondary victim of violent crime will ever achieve."[1] He makes this statement after living a life defined by the 1958 murder of his mother, which remains unsolved to this day.

What Mr. Ellroy says might be true. Still, I pray that the Madison and Smalley families will be blessed some day with closure of one form or another.

In 1990, Ida Madison told *The Dallas Morning News*, "Even if my daughter is dead, I want to know what happened to her. I just know in my heart that there is somebody somewhere who knows what happened to them."[2]

I have no doubt that Ida Madison is correct. There is at minimum one person who knows how and why Stacie and Susan died and whose hands are stained with their blood. It is obscene that these individuals have not come forward before now.

TIME FOR OTHERS TO FINALLY SPEAK UP AS WELL

It is also time for another group to finally speak up about what they know. These people are Stacie's and Susan's friends and acquaintances who, although they most likely do not know the girls' final fates, have withheld other information that may be vital to solving this mystery.

It will no doubt be adjudged controversial, but I contend that there are people known to the girls who, for any number of reasons, have not been completely forthcoming with what they know (or even suspect) regarding March 20, 1988. I base this claim upon subtle but troubling truths of which I became aware in the course of pursuing this book project.

---

1 Murder by the Book, Court TV, November 14, 2006.
2 *The Dallas Morning News*, March 15, 1990.

FEAR OF BEING LABELED A GOSSIP?

For one thing, I located numerous people via the internet's various online communities who knew Stacie and Susan. When notified by me of my intention to write this book, I was fortunate to discover that most of them were only too happy to answer my questions about the girls. Many were likewise willing to allow me to use statements they had previously posted online regarding Stacie and Susan.

However, although they were thankfully in the slimmest of minorities, I also discovered a small number of people who were uncomfortable speaking with me. The reasons they offered for refusing my requests for information were variations on the same theme. Specifically, they were apprehensive out of fear of being accused by others of "bad mouthing" Stacie and Susan.

Initially, I paid little attention to these comments, given that the majority of people whom I approached had been so gracious to me. Yet as time wore on, I grew increasingly troubled by the term "bad mouthing." For one thing, I had stressed to everyone I encountered that it was my intention to emphasize the positive in this story as often as possible. I never once asked anyone to provide me with any form of gossip.

My question then became, "Just what is it these people know?" Were they fearful of sharing what they know about the disappearances of the girls because in doing so they would have to reveal that they were partying with or near Stacie and Susan on March 20, 1988? I also wondered, "Who has withheld information for all these years regarding Stacie and Susan for fear that they too might be perceived as 'bad mouthing' the girls? From whom have they hidden what they know about March 20, 1988 and why?"

Granted, I quickly came to realize that the reputations with which these people are concerned in 2009 are not those of Stacie and Susan, but instead their own. They are fearful that, by revealing whatever it is they knew about that night, their own legacies might suffer. This struck me as the ultimate in selfishness.

After nearly 22 years, could they possibly possess any knowledge about Stacie and Susan that would go beyond the typical juvenile behavior in which nearly all teenagers engage at one time or another? Moreover, considering that the girls are long presumed dead, would these people have anything to offer that could be more hurtful to the Madison and Smalley families than living through an unsolved nightmare for two decades?

NO SPECULATION OF ANY KIND EVER OFFERED

What I found equally disturbing – especially in light of this

145

incomprehensible fear that some people seemed to have of being branded a gossip in scenario involving two dead girls – was the realization that, in the near 22 years since they disappeared, not one single person known to the girls has ever come forward to offer so much as substantive speculation regarding where Stacie and Susan may have been heading on the night they vanished, any intimation as to what the girls' intentions for being out and about so late were, or even a prediction as to who they might have met on Forest Lane. Was this just mere coincidence or is the silence intentional?

Ida Madison says Stacie's closest friend, Heidi Monk Wilhelm, told her that she "didn't believe for a minute that Stacie got into a car with someone she didn't know, unless Susan knew them."

Moreover, Ida stated:

> Heidi and Stacie were cruising Forest Lane one night and two older men - translate that to college age - pulled up next to them and offered to give them some beer if they would ride with them...Heidi and Stacie looked at each other and said, "Let's get out of here," and they did.[3]

As well, as Deanna Bowman Sinclair told me, "I think that Stacie and Susan had to know who they were meeting," and Carolyn Smalley said, "All indications appear it was someone they knew."[4]

In this regard, Ohlen Sapp offered the observation that, even at 2:00 a.m. on a Sunday morning, Forest Lane was a very busy place on the weekends. So, he believes, it is highly unlikely that one girl, let alone two, would enter a stranger's vehicle against their will, without a fight and in utter silence on such an active street.[5]

Accordingly, we must presume Stacie and Susan parked their car at the intersection of Webbs Chapel Road and Forest Lane in order to accept a ride from someone they knew to one degree or another.

In any event, based upon the above assertions, the presumption can only be that the girls entered a vehicle owned by someone they knew and trusted to one degree or another. More than likely, they knew the driver of this car very well.

WHO WAS THIS MYSTERY DRIVER?

The reader is cautioned to realize that the person from whom Stacie and Susan accepted this ride might not necessarily be the

---

3 Ida Madison, June 18, 2009.
4 Deanna Bowman Sinclair, October 1, 2009 and Carolyn Smalley, September 22, 2009.
5 Ohlen Sapp, October 17, 2009.

same individual responsible for their deaths. There is no question, however, that the girls were taken somewhere by this person and in a car other than their own.

Perhaps it was to an all night restaurant, a party at a friend's house, a gathering at one of the lakes in the Dallas area, or to a remote cemetery near a fish hatchery. At that location, provided they were not already in their company, the girls met the person or persons who murdered them.

Granted, this mystery driver might not be able to answer the ultimate question regarding what became of the girls, but they might possibly be the missing link in the chain of events that does lead to a resolution.

The point is that someone other than Stacie and Susan drove the girls to the unknown destination to which they headed when they left Webbs Chapel Road and Forest Lane on that March night so many years ago. I assert that people known to the girls either know or suspect who this person was.

When I spoke with Ida Madison regarding the possibility that there may be people out there who have not been completely forthcoming with what they know or suspect out of fear of being labeled a gossip or a traitor of some sort, her response was:

> I had never thought about this angle...withholding a vital clue to protect their own reputation. Who cares after 21 years what they [the people withholding information] did when they were 17 or 18, unless they were the murderer or with that person? The utter audacity of such behavior floors me! Many of the people who knew Stacie and/or Susan need to take a long hard look at the other people they knew at this time. Are their own kids now playing or going out with the kids of some of those people? What do they really know about those people as parents? Could their precious child be hanging out in the home of a murderer?[6]

Ida is correct on all counts. Unquestionably, not everyone has shared everything they know or suspect with police, and their justifications for doing so are absurd.

SOMEBODY SOMEWHERE KNOWS

In 1990, Ida Madison stated to the press, "I just know in my heart that there is somebody somewhere who knows what happened to them [Stacie and Susan], and I want them to know that they have put

---

6 Ida Madison, August 10, 2009.

us through pure hell."[7] To this day, she stands by this conviction and insists that the only way the mystery of Stacie's and Susan's disappearances will ever be solved will be by "getting that one person who knows something to come forward."[8]

Now is the time for that someone to examine their conscience, do the right thing, and finally speak up regarding what they know.

---

7 *The Dallas Morning News*, March 15, 1990.
8 Id. and Ida Madison, June 6, 2009.

20

ALTERNATE REALITIES

What if Stacie and Susan had opted to stay at
the Smalley condominium when they returned to it?

As a student of history, I enjoy pondering alternate realities.

Had John F. Kennedy not died in 1963, would the war in Vietnam have become the quagmire that it did under Lyndon B. Johnson?

Would the film *Raiders of the Lost Ark* have been the success it was had Steven Spielberg been able to cast Tom Selleck in the role of Indiana Jones, as he had originally hoped to do?

Would Sharon Tate still be alive had Charles Manson been signed to a recording contract in 1968?

What would music sound like today had John Lennon never met Paul McCartney?

WHAT IF?

Since undertaking this project, my mind has turned repeatedly to "What if Stacie and Susan had opted to stay at the Smalley condominium when they returned to it from Arlington in the hours past midnight on Sunday, March 20, 1988?" Or, to lay blame where it actually belongs, "What if the monster responsible for the girls' disappearances had found a droplet of humanity inside his soul and allowed the girls to go on with their lives?"

The concept is overwhelming.

MARRIED WITH CHILDREN?

Were she still with them, Susan Smalley's family would have celebrated her 40th birthday in September 2009. Readying herself to pass that milestone, Susan might have good naturedly dreaded the grief she knew would be coming her way from her still 39 year old friend Stacie Madison.

Obviously, 21 years after graduation, although communication with old friends is easier in this day of MySpace and Facebook, the girls might well have lost touch with one another years ago, and one might be saying of the other, "Wow! I have not thought about that girl in years!"

The safe bet is that, with their personalities, the girls' surnames would no longer be "Smalley" or "Madison." Instead, they would no doubt be married, hopefully to men who treat them with the respect they deserve. Or, as some are prone to do, perhaps they would have made a few mistakes in love before getting it right. The possibilities are endless. The important thing, above all else, is that the girls would still be here and living their lives.

Susan, Carolyn Smalley told me, loved children and dreamed of having several of her own. Perhaps she might be living that dream today.

Stacie would also most likely be raising children of her own while also pursuing a career.

What is dumbfounding in this regard is the reality that the girls' children today would probably be teenagers themselves and close to the ages Stacie and Susan were when they disappeared two decades ago.

Stacie's immediate dream in 1988 was geared towards going to college, studying business, and becoming a businesswoman. Had she been allowed to pursue that dream, in a "local girl makes good" moment, Stacie's name today might be as well known as Mary Kay Ash or Ebby Halliday. We will never know.

PRESENT FOR MILESTONE EVENTS

In reality, had Stacie and Susan returned home to their families on that Sunday in March so long ago, and had the girls been left to pursue their dreams, they would most likely be what the majority of us are - anonymous and unknown entities in society. They would today be but two of the thousands of students who have graduated from Newman Smith High School since its doors were opened, and their names and faces would be known only to their families, friends and co-workers. Having talked to the Madison and Smalley families, I know that none of this would matter to them. They would be happy just to have the girls among them whatever the circumstances might be.

Had the girls not vanished in 1988, their loved ones would not have been forced to hear about the girls on television in 1988 or read about them in print for years thereafter. The Facebook group created in the girls' memory would not exist, and there would have been no need for this book to have been written. All of this the families would have welcomed.

The Madisons and Smalleys would have also welcomed the girls at milestone events in their respective families' lives. Case in point, the Madisons, who once erected as many as three Christmas trees inside their home in December and who used to go out trick or treating as a family at Halloween, have never truly "celebrated" a holiday since 1988.

THIS IS REALITY

In 1990, two years after Stacie's disappearances, Ida Madison told a reporter for *The Dallas Morning News*, "[T]here is somebody somewhere who knows what happened to [Stacie and Susan], and I want them to know that they have put us through pure hell."[1]

For Ida, this feeling was compounded in 1996, eight years after Stacie's disappearance, when her husband died from cancer. In turn, following her husband's death, Ida was forced to move into the next phase of her life without one of her three children there to comfort her.

Equally distressing about Frank Madison's death is the reality that the man's eyes closed on this life without his firstborn by his side and without a resolution regarding what had become of her. Until the day of his death, says Ida Madison, her husband had never really been able to move beyond the initial sorrow and grief that comes to a father who has lost a child.[2]

Sadly, this is reality.

A CAREFREE SUMMER

But this section is about alternate realities, and I choose to end it by painting for the reader a mental portrait of two girls who return to the Smalley household safe and sound well before sunrise on March 20, 1988, collapse into bed from exhaustion, and then sleep past noon.

The next day, Monday, March 21, 1988, after an uneventful Spring Break, they resume what remains of their senior year at Newman Smith High School.

Less than three months later, they walk across the stage at their high school graduation and receive their diplomas with honors. Thereafter, but before they begin their days at college, the girls will spend their summer simply enjoying the fact that they are young and carefree.

AS GOD INTENDED IT TO BE

In 2001, Michael Granberry wrote that Susan "wanted to graduate and head to Florida, with her mother riding beside her in the brand-

---

1 *The Dallas Morning News*, March 15, 1990.
2 Ida Madison, June 20, 2009.

new car she couldn't wait to buy."[3]

When speaking with Carolyn Smalley of their plans for that summer, she said that she and Susan had spoken often of traveling to Florida for a vacation just to go somewhere, especially to a place that involved a view of the ocean.[4]

In my alternate reality, I envision the car of Susan's choice being a sporty convertible, probably red, the kind that eats you alive in insurance payments.

On a hot summer's day, Susan and Carolyn Smalley travel down the highway at speeds that exceed the posted limit.

As they near the Florida coast, the winds blow back Susan's hair. She will definitely have to wash it once they reach their destination.

Thoughts of primping make Susan's mind run towards thoughts of her friend Stacie Madison – "Miss America".

Susan will have to send Stacie a postcard telling her all about the things she and her mother plan to do while they are in the Sunshine State.

Stacie, with her plans to go to college in Denton, has a new boyfriend – one far less complicated than her last one. She is spending her summer taking on more responsibility at the doctor's office where she works. Stacie's bosses are grooming her to become their office manager, whether she realizes it or not.

Susan too has a job waiting for her once this vacation is over. She is, in truth, still working both jobs. But this is all for another day.

She will be back in Dallas soon enough, working and going to school once more. There will be plenty of time for all of that.

This week is all about fun.

So, she shifts the car into high gear, as she speaks to her mother of all the things she hopes to do in the coming months and years.

She, as is Stacie, is precisely what God intends for her to be right now: a vibrant and healthy young girl with her entire life in front of her and so many dreams for the future she does not know which ones to pursue first.

In an alternate reality…

---

3 *The Dallas Morning News*, August 19, 2001.
4 Id.

21

IF I HAD ONE MORE CHANCE

Towards the end of 1988, Ida Madison sat down at the computer on which Stacie had once done her homework assignments and typed a letter to the daughter she anticipated she would never see again. That letter was subsequently published in an article written by Laura Miller, the future mayor of Dallas, in a December 1988 edition of *The Dallas Times Herald*. It is re-printed here in its entirety.

Dear Stacie:

There are so many things I would tell you if I had one more chance to talk to you. There are so many things that have happened since I last kissed you good-bye. Some good, some not so good.

Your little sister Stefanie has started the first grade and has written many times in her journal of her sister, Stacie. She thinks and talks of you often. She broke her arm two weeks after school started and wished you could sign her cast. Her arm has healed; her heart hasn't. Sara is having a successful year in 8th grade. She has made the honor roll for the first time in her attempts to live up to your example.

Your best friend Heidi misses you too. She is in college and pursuing the love you both shared – baton twirling. She too has things she wishes she could share with you.

Your grandmother has prayed long and often for your return or a resolution to our grief. She is not looking forward to Christmas without you.

Your Dad and I have attempted to go on with our lives because it seems to be the only thing we can do. But it has never been easy. Every day is as difficult as the one before with no ending in sight. We pray that you are alive and well even though that seems most unlikely. We pray that if you are not, that you are in the loving arms of God, and that some day we will see you again.

Above all else we would want you to know that we will always love you.[1]

---

1 Laura Miller, "Daughter's disappearance still lingers," *The Dallas Times Herald*, December 5, 1988.

BIBLIOGRAPHY

ARTICLES

Barber, Dan R., "Still without a clue: parents, school recall girls missing since '88," *The Dallas Morning News,* March 14, 1992.

"Carrollton folk celebrate start of sewer system," *The Dallas Morning News*, July 13, 1928.

"Carrollton to get traffic signal light," *The Carrollton Chronicle*, September 10, 1937.

Ellroy, James, *"The Haunting."* Newsweek, August 10 & 17, 2009, p. 44.

Everback, Tracy, "Carrollton police ask for help in finding 2 missing teen-agers," *The Dallas Morning News*, March 24, 1988.

Granberry, Michael, "Vanished without a trace – 13 years after teens disappeared, families still wait, wonder," *The Dallas Morning News*, August 19, 2001.

Jackson, Kathy, "'This is just a heart-rending situation': no clues found in search for missing teens; friends fear worst," *The Dallas Morning News*, March 25, 1988.

Jackson, Kathy, "Moms cling to hope for 2 missing teens," *The Dallas Morning News*, March 30, 1988.

Jackson, Kathy, "Clinging to hope: with no new leads in Carrolton teens' disappearance, parents fear worst," *The Dallas Morning News*, May 15, 1988.

Jackson, Kathy, "Leads are few a year after teens vanished," *The Dallas Morning News*, March 20, 1989

"Little revealed in decade since 2 teens vanished," *The Fort Worth Star-Telegram*, March 18, 1998.

"The Lion's Tale slashes onto stage," *The Dallas Morning News*, October 5, 1934.

"Metro Report," *The Dallas Morning News*, March 26, 1988.

Miller, Bobbi, "Missing students recalled: posters, ribbons urge spring break caution," *The Dallas Morning News*, March 15, 1990.

Miller, Laura, "Missing girl's world waiting for her return," *The Dallas Times Herald*, March 30, 1988.

Miller, Laura, "Daughter's disappearance still lingers," *The Dallas Times Herald*, December 5, 1988.

"Rites set for area schoolman," *The Dallas Morning News*, June 12, 1962.

"Students keep the faith," *The Dallas Morning News*, May 28, 1988.

Swindle, Kathy, "Children are always worth a celebration," *The Dallas Morning News*, March 19, 1996.

BOOKS

Doyle, Arthur Conan, "The Red-headed League," *The Complete Sherlock Holmes, Volume 1*, Barnes & Noble Classics, 2004, p. 215.

Simon, David, *Homicide: A Year on the Killing Streets*, Houghton Mifflin, 1991, p. 73.

Wolfe, Thomas, *Of Time and the River,* Charles Scribner's Sons, 1935, p. 460.

TELEVISION PROGRAMS

Murder by the Book, Court TV, November 14, 2006.

WEBSITES

http://cfbstaff.cfbisd.edu

http://www.cityofcarrollton.com

INTERVIEWS

David W. Bock, October 17, 2009.

John W. Crawford, June 4, 2009.

"Jason Lawton," July 15, 2009 and November 3, 2009.

Ida Madison, June 20, 2009.

Stefanie Madison, June 20, 2009.

"Avis Morgan," September 29, 2009, October 13, 2009 and November 4, 2009.

Joel Payne, November 3, 2009 and November 9, 2009.

Joe Pouncy, September 18, 2009.

Ohlen L. Sapp, October 17, 2009.

Carolyn Smalley, July 14, 2009.

John Richard Smalley, July 5, 2009.

Rich Smalley, June 27, 2009 and July 14, 2009.

Greg Ward, June 16, 2009.

ELECTRONIC MAIL

Many of the quotations used in this book are derived from electronic mail exchanges between the author and the various individuals quoted. Given the cumbersome number of these exchanges, they have been neither catalogued nor incorporated into this bibliography.

ABOUT THE AUTHOR

Shawn Sutherland is a graduate of Newman Smith High School and Abilene Christian University. He lives in the Dallas, Texas area, where he has been involved in patent law for the past 16 years.

His articles on cults have been published by the International Cultic Studies Association and the Jonestown Institute.

He is currently at work on *Barefoot Messiah of the Atomic Age*, the definitive biography of Francis H. Pencovic who, prior to reinventing himself in the 1940s as messiah and cult leader Krishna Venta, had been a burglar, confidence man, convict and soldier.

This Night Wounds Time: The Mysterious Disappearances of Stacie Madison and Susan Smalley is his first book.

4411403

Made in the USA
Lexington, KY
22 January 2010